7 Days of Christmas

Nicole Dennis

A homeless orphan finds a small town and someone to show him the magic of the holidays with seven red envelopes.

. . . . .

ON THE 7TH DAY OF CHRISTMAS, my Safe Haven gave to me - *The Warmth of the Season.*

On the 6th Day of Christmas, my Safe Haven gave to me - *A Fresh Start of the Season.*

On the 5th Day of Christmas, my Safe Haven gave to me - *Rags to Riches of the Season.*

On the 4th Day of Christmas, my Safe Haven gave to me - *The Wonderful Scent of the Season.*

On the 3rd Day of Christmas, my Safe Haven gave to me - *A Christmas Season to Believe In.*

On the 2nd Day of Christmas, my One Hope gave to me - *Surprises of the Season!*

On the 1st Day of Christmas, my One Hope gave to me - *Visions of the Season!*

7 Days of Christmas is a work of fiction. Names, characters, places, and incidents are the products of the author's imagination or are used fictitiously. Any resemblance to actual events, locales, or persons, living or dead, is entirely coincidental.

A Note from the Author

If you did not purchased this book from an authorized retailer you make it difficult for me to write the next book. Please stop any and all piracy and purchase the book. For all those who purchased the book legitimately: Thank you! Please – share the word and promise no more piracy.

3rd Ebook Publication & Copyright © December 2022 by FatCat Books Ink

Edits – Kris Jacen www.krisjacen.com/three-hearts

Cover design – FatCat Books Ink
Attention Readers: This book uses US English.

The author acknowledges the trademarked status and owners of the following word marks used in this story:

Starbucks: *Starbucks, Inc.*

Dark Hunters: *Sherrilyn Kenyon*

Ben & Jerry's: *Ben & Jerry's Homemade, Inc.*

iPhone/iPod: *Apple, Inc.*

Soul: *Kia Motors America, Inc.*

Dockers: *Levi Strauss and Company*

Crock-Pot: *Sunbeam Products, Inc.*

It's a Wonderful Life: *RKO Radio Pictures*

How the Grinch Stole Christmas: *Dr. Seuss Enterprises, L.P. Geisel-Seuss Enterprises, Inc.*

Chapter One

Ever since he phased out of the foster system at eighteen, things hadn't been going his way.

Noel Hudson did everything he was supposed to while trying to make his way in the world. He managed to get decent grades up through high school, but found it harder to maintain them while being shoved from one foster home to another, to a group home and back. Each time he had to toss his things into garbage bags to shlep to the next place. He felt like he was a number on the roulette wheel when all he wanted one place to say and finish school. It didn't happen, so he barely made the grades to graduate. He couldn't qualify for any type of scholarships or grants, not even with his foster status.

No. Instead of a chance at higher education, he was left to join the rat race with thousands of others more qualified than he was. Boston was the same as any other city. Somehow, he managed to get two minimum-wage jobs.

Rushing from one position to the other, he pulled together enough money to rent a single bedroom suite in an old building. It was no better than a flophouse, but he could lock up his basic things, get on a bicycle, and reach both jobs. While he didn't have any extras, he had a mattress to sleep on, a bathroom, heat and lights, and food. Thanks to the state, he managed to qualify for both food assistance and medical care to receive his insulin and diabetes paraphernalia that kept his sugars regulated. With the small amount of food stamps, he could purchase a little more than peanut butter and jelly sandwiches, the ramen noodle soup, and the cheap coffee he lived on when the allotment ran out. At times, he could bring home fresh, healthy items and tried to stretch out everything. He stored what he could in the tiny fridge, plastic cartons became his pantry, and he had a microwave and hot plate to cook everything. He learned how to stretch every dollar and kept a strict budget. No fun, no extras, and no free days kept him in his room and fed.

For three years and different minimum-wage jobs, Noel managed to keep his head above the water and his butt in the little room. It wasn't much, but he accomplished everything on his own and made it work.

Until that last winter season, four years ago, he watched the snowstorms turned into blizzard after blizzard. The ancient heater barely kept the chill out of the room. He tried to move the mattress in front of it, but it didn't help. He wore multiple layers and rolled in blankets, but it didn't help him from chattering and shivering throughout the night. Since he didn't have extra funds for public transportation, he relied on his bicycle to get to and from work, when it made it through the streets. If he couldn't use it, he walked the miles.

The problems started with a simple cough and runny nose. He grabbed the cheapest medicine to counteract it. The cough deepened, rattling through his lungs.

During his last shift of the week, he collapsed, caught in a high fever, bone-aching chills, and a deepening phlegmy cough filled with icky mucus. Complications with his juvenile Type-1 diabetes weakened his immune system and he succumbed to bacterial pneumonia. It knocked him flat on his ass and into a hospital bed.

For weeks.

When he finally left, not fully recovered but able to breathe on his own and the occasional help from an inhaler, he tried to go back to his reality.

It was too late.

The managers hired a new person at both jobs. There was nothing else for him. Since he had been in those last two jobs for only six months, neither one gave him worker's compensation or unemployment benefits. He was on his own. He searched for another solid week, but no one was hiring in the deep winter.

A week later, he lost his electricity, heat, and his room. He used the last couple of hours to pack what precious belongings, blankets, and clothes he could into the canvas seabag. His diabetes stuff and other personal stuff remained in the messenger bag he fixed with duct tape. He managed to scrounge both of them at the thrift store along with some other clothes.

A kind nurse, Lenora, gave him a heavy pea coat, scarf, woolen hat, gloves, and boots before he left. She pressed whatever cash she had in her pocket into his hands. He had a few of those dollars left. It wasn't enough to pay off his bills until a new job came along.

Broke, jobless, and homeless, Noel tried to figure out how to navigate life on the streets. With the bitter cold growing, good people around the city opened multiple shelters to take in those who had nowhere else to go. Noel found a bed at one of them, assisted around the shelter to keep it until it closed.

During the first year of being homeless, he struggled as he learned to survive every day in the face of not having access to the necessities for hygiene. He figured out how to move around, find food and water, and somewhere to sleep. Like all the other homeless, he became another nameless face. Condemned buildings were his favorite sleeping spots, but gangs and locals claimed many of them. Sometimes he found a clump of bushes. Another frightening time was sleeping inside a cardboard box at the end of an alley.

For the next three years, he became more adept at living on the street, maintaining the quiet status, not causing any type of trouble or pulling attention to himself. He panhandled when he could. Found the occasional odd job for a bit of money. Knew which places would give him leftovers after a shift or fed the homeless.

One of his lucky moments happened when he discovered a discarded tent next to a sports store; he pulled it out and managed to fix it. With the tent, he could keep out the elements. It collapsed into a roll attached to his seabag. He used it to hide in the small forests scattered in the various parks and camouflage his hiding spots to protect himself. In the daytime, he broke down the tent, changed what clothes he could, and used one of multiple spots to stash the seabag for the day. He kept his messenger bag and bike when he headed back into the city.

Some days he spent in the library after a quick wash in an open restroom and change of shirts to remove most of the stink. Oh, how he loved spending days in the library, tons of books at hand, and he could disappear for hours. He had a bathroom and water fountain to use when he needed.

After the first few weeks, the head librarian, Sarah, came to recognize him and often brought him a bagged lunch or some extra money. She got him on the computer where he could search for possible jobs or another location to sleep. They became friends over the years, with Sarah often giving him a bag of clothes, necessities, or a supply of food to keep him going. Those packages were the best kind of presents and he treasured all of them.

When he left the library and walked outside to unlock his bike for the trip, he made the mistake of crossing in front of one of the local gangs that controlled the area. They saw him and crowded him back into the closest alleyway.

"Little homeless fag. What are you doing all alone? Hmm? No daddy to keep you in his bed? No fuck buddy," the leader said as he shoved Noel back into the wall.

Noel kept his eyes on the ground so as not to confront the bastard. He knew never to argue with one of the gangs. He had learned the hard way. One night several gang members beat him to the ground when he let his words fly out without a filter. "Please, let me leave."

"Not this time, little homo. You cross our streets way too much. You act like you're better than the other homeless. Homeless are shit.

Worse than our druggies. You're shit on the ground, li'l homo," the leader said, punching Noel's shoulder. He dug his fingers into Noel's chest. "This is our turf."

"I'm not interested in your turf. I only pass through here to visit the library."

"What do you want in that sissy place?"

"It's somewhere to stay. It's all I want."

"I don't like your presence on my street. Having shit on the sidewalk scares away my customers. You owe me. You need to pay up."

"I'm sorry, but I don't know anything about clients not finding your spot," Noel said, knowing he didn't do anything to scare drug addicts from scoring a fix.

"Do you want a hit? I can give you a hit of something pure." The leader snapped his fingers and one of his boys shoved a packet in his hand. He rolled the packet between his thick fingers.

Noel didn't even look at the packet. He wouldn't go near that stuff. "No, thank you. I don't use drugs."

"Too good to take a hit? It's so sweet the first time."

"No money to pay for them if I did use them."

"You can afford them. Get on your knees."

Noel felt his heart thump harder. He'd tried this once when he was desperate for food. It didn't end well. He'd barfed.

"Did ya hear me? Get on your knees, sissy. I want your mouth."

Noel shook his head.

"Get on your knees!" the punk roared.

Noel didn't see what hit him across the head. It knocked everything out of him, so he collapsed on the ground at the mercy of their boots. He rolled as best he could until it was over. He had no memory of what happened until Sarah found him and dialed 911.

His former nurse, Lenora, found him in the ER. Diagnosed with bruised ribs, pissing blood, and a concussion, he was a mess. That had nothing to do with his unkempt appearance.

Lenora asked the doctor to run some diagnostic testing on his diabetes and he grimaced. Sure enough, the doctor admitted him after he discovered his dangerous insulin levels. He wasn't eating enough to counteract the medication and the damage continued to work his system.

Under her careful watch, she made sure he ate the nutritious meals he needed as a diabetic, tested his sugars, and administered the insulin. He could rest, take a shower when he could move, and recover.

Both Lenora and Sarah collected donated clothes, sustainable food that didn't rot or interfere with the insulin, and funds. Before the hospital released him, Lenora and Sarah visited him. He knew it wasn't to wish him well. He saw it in their gazes.

"Look, baby, autumn is almost over. Winter will be upon us soon. You can't survive another harsh winter on the streets. If you develop pneumonia again, it could kill you," Lenora said.

"There's no other choice," Noel said as he fiddled with the blanket. "The last time I was in here, I lost everything I managed to scrape together. A pitiful room, food, and power were all I had and they're gone. I worked eighteen-hour days between two different places. I don't have the education or skills."

"You can't return to the streets, certainly not by the library. If that gang sees you again, they'll kill you," Sarah said.

"Can I go to another branch to hide?"

"I only work at that one and I spoke with the other two branches. Neither were in safe territory."

"I'll find somewhere else to go," he said. "I managed to survive four years on the streets, I'll continue to make the best of it."

"We believe you need to go somewhere else. Out of Boston and the northeast. You can't survive here."

"I can't survive anywhere. Not since I was left as a newborn in a hospital. I shouldn't have lived back then." Noel closed his eyes and swallowed several times.

"I have a friend who lives in Baltimore. He can give you a place to stay," Sarah said. "It gets knocked with storms, but you can survive there. You can find a job and start over."

"How would I get there? I can't ride my bike."

"Oh no, I thought you knew," Lenora said.

"Know what?"

Sarah sighed as she looked to Lenora and then Noel. "When I got to you, your bike was gone, even the chain and lock. They stole it."

Noel groaned. "Great. My one mode of transportation is gone."

"Noel, take this chance. Please."

There was no other choice. He nodded.

When he left the hospital, he spent a couple of days with Sarah at her home. She helped him retrieve his things from the woods. They salvaged what they could from his clothes and sent them through the wash cycle multiple times. She took him shopping to replenish the necessities, adding to what she gathered with Lenora and insisted on helping him build up his clothing. When he couldn't stop her, he told her only go to the thrift stores. They were good enough for him. He refused to let her spend everything on him. As he repacked the bag with the clean and new items, he didn't give up the last few tattered paperback copies of the Harry Potter series, notebooks, pens, and an old radio he stashed deep inside the seabag. He kept an old battered watch one of his foster fathers had given him after receiving a brand new classy one.

Lenora made sure to give him additional boxes of needles, test strips, and bottles of insulin for the trip. Neither one was sure when he would find a free clinic to give him the supplies he needed to survive. A day or two without his insulin and he would either fall into a coma or die.

One week later, he climbed the bus with his seabag, tent, and messenger bag. He waved to Lenora and Sarah as he found his seat.

Still exhausted from his earlier injuries, he slept most of the way down. He left the bus with his things when it stopped in Wilmington on Seventh Street. He stretched his legs and entered the small store to purchase water and a sandwich. He walked across the street to the riverfront park and found a tree. Settling underneath it, he ate the simple meal, people-watched, and enjoyed the sun. There was a crisp scent and feel to the breeze as the days drew closer to Thanksgiving. He hadn't expected to fall asleep again.

When he woke and raced back to the station, the bus was gone. The lady said there wouldn't be another until tomorrow and his ticket would be invalid for the trip.

Devastated at the lost opportunity, Noel didn't dare call Sarah to tell her how he messed up. She and Lenora had already done so much for him. He would have to figure out what to do without more help. He could do it. He knew how.

At least this place was new.

He took several free maps of the area and went outside to find a park and sit. There, he pulled out his pen and notebook and opened the maps. He marked down places where he could sleep, find food, libraries, malls, and even a church or two. He circled a couple of gay-friendly spots.

He spotted a town called Blackbourne River north and west of Wilmington along the Brandywine Creek. If he worked his way over there, perhaps taking time to find a job or two raking leaves or other things for some extra cash, he could reach it before mid-December. Two gay-friendly hostels were on the way.

He could do this.

"Blackbourne River. New place. New chance."

With the plan set in his head, he packed everything in his messenger bag. He walked away from the park and to the river. Before he left the city, he stopped at a grocery store to gather what food and water he could to survive the walking trip. He added one of those insulated pouches to keep the water and some fresh food cool. The long strap allowed him to sling it over his shoulder with the rest of his belongings.

"Looks like you're on a bit of an outdoor adventure," the cashier said while she rung him up.

After he got out his wallet, he carefully counted the cash and change to see what he could afford and didn't need. "Something like that," he said. "A new start at life."

"Good for you. Sometimes each one of us needs to let go of everything and have a restart," she said.

When the total came up, it was more than what he wanted to spend. He looked through the items to see what he could put back. "You know. I don't need these..."

"Oh, I forgot your coupons. I'm so sorry," she said.

"Coupons?"

"Hmm. Lemme go through them," she said and pulled out a couple of packets of paper. She ripped out several from each packet and scanned them in.

Noel watched the total drop below what he wanted and he could keep everything. "Thank you," he whispered, tears in his eyes.

"Sometimes we each need a break in life. Can you afford this?"

He nodded and handed over the carefully counted cash and change. "What do you know about Blackbourne River?"

"The little town set again Brandywine Creek?"

Noel nodded.

"I love it. It has this great old-time downtown shopping center. They have tree-lighting ceremonies, snowman contests, and even snowball fights. It's magical. A great drive from the city along the river and historical forest."

Noel grimaced about all the holiday crap. He never celebrated the holiday, which followed his nonexistent birthday. Even when he had been in foster or group homes, he never got the idea of celebrating all of these holidays. They were just another day to him.

The cashier smiled as she continued to describe the town and said, "December seems a little chillier up there, which is wonderful this time of the year."

"Do they welcome newcomers?"

"Do you mean down-on-their-luck newcomers who need a chance?"

Noel nodded.

"Yes, they're warm and open." The lady looked at him again. "Do you like books?"

Noel dropped his mouth open. "I love them. I used to spend most of my days in a library up north."

"When you get there, find a store called BookWorm. You can't miss it. Something could happen there."

As he thought about her words, Noel packed the paper and pantry items in the seabag. The cashier exchanged his warm cold pack for one that had been in the freezer to keep his items cold.

He looked at her and smiled. "Thank you for everything."

"Good luck and take care." She waved again. "Perhaps I'll see you at the BookWorm."

"I will and I hope so too," Noel said as he waved and left the store. He felt much better about his destination.

Outside, he adjusted all of the bags to hang in balanced positions. He moved the new-for-him pea coat under the bags. He tugged the woolen fedora from the seabag and shoved it on his head. He pulled the brim down.

Next, he checked the map and got his bearings. With his path laid out, he started walking.

Chapter Two

There he was again, standing on the opposite side of the street.

Justin Llewellyn made his way along the sidewalk to his shop; car keys jangled in his fingers, and a Starbucks carrier and bag balanced in his other hand. A late-night storm made the sidewalks a touch icy this early in the morning. He stopped to study the young man for a few moments. He couldn't keep himself from locating the stranger. He was easy to pick out in the same pea coat, thinned and battered as if someone had tossed it away. It didn't do much to protect the slender frame against the biting cold winds. Luckily, the heavier snows would hold off for another week or so, but then it would get worse for him.

Justin figured him for one of the young homeless kids who seemed to move between Philadelphia, Wilmington, and Baltimore as if following Interstate 95.

Along with the pea coat, the kid clutched the strap of a duct-taped messenger bag slung across his body with a fingerless-gloved hand. A wool-felt fedora pulled low over his face to protect it from the bitter wind. When he turned to the side, Justin saw the same old canvas seabag hanging across his back. He realized the bag was one of those a sailor or soldier carried. It was at that point Justin figured out this kid carried his entire existence in that bag.

Every morning for the last two weeks, this young man — perhaps no more than a teenager — had waited for Justin to open his store, BookWorm, where he sat and read quietly in one of the leather armchairs for almost the entire day.

With the weather pattern about to become worse, Justin decided he would learn everything he could about the boy this morning. He opened the locks for what would be the busiest holiday rush as they counted down the last eight days to Christmas. He needed a good season to keep his business in the black, like all the other small businesses within the quaint, old-fashioned town of Blackbourne River. He felt the strap of his laptop bag slip as he juggled everything to get inside.

"Crap. Hell."

"Hang on, I got it." Fingerless-gloved hands took the coffee carrier and paper bag.

His helper was the young man. Somehow, the kid had raced across the street to assist him. The kid was older than he thought, maybe in his early to mid-twenties.

"Hi, thanks for the extra hand. I thought everything would crash to the ground there for a moment. That wouldn't be a good thing. I need my caffeine." He shrugged the shoulder strap back in place, shoved the key in the lock, and pushed the door open. As they both straightened, Justin noticed the kid was a couple of inches shorter than his six-foot frame. He waved the young man in first. "Are you coming in for the day?"

The kid ducked his head and stepped inside the warm store.

Justin followed him, flipped on the lights, but not the sign. There were two more hours before he opened, even for the holiday season. Instead of working on the usual paperwork, he wanted the chance to get some answers out of his mysterious visitor.

After two weeks of building curiosity and a little bit of intrigue, he wondered who this kid was. Every day, this young stranger sat quietly in his store reading, drank from a bottle of water he refilled from the bathroom sink, ate peanut butter and jelly sandwiches, and purchased nothing. There was an air of hopelessness surrounding him as the days became darker. If anyone needed help during the Christmas season, this fragile looking kid was at the top of Justin's personal list. Growing up with wealth behind his name amongst the Washington DC elite, he learned from his grandparents to never look down upon anyone and give whenever he could. He should give his time or support something. There was no way he forgot those instructions. Unwinding the red and blue striped scarf from his neck, he led the young man to the leather chairs gathered around a low wooden coffee table.

"You don't mind me coming in before you open?"

"It's too damn cold to leave you standing outside." Justin waved a hand as he took the carrier and bag after dropping his things on one of the chairs. "Besides, I don't mind the company."

"Thanks, appreciate it, sir." He bypassed the chairs and headed to the shelves to find the book he was reading yesterday. He recently started the *Dark Hunters* series by Sherrilyn Kenyon and seemed to enjoy them by the speed he moved through the books.

"I'm not a sir. Someone calls me 'sir' and I look around for my father. I would be shocked down to my socks, since I would never find my father in Blackbourne River. He's a DC man born and bred and doesn't leave his stomping grounds. Call me Justin."

"Okay, thanks, Justin then."

Justin grumbled when he didn't get a name in return, but hoped his next offer might loosen the tension. "I hope you like hot chocolate and blueberry scones. I wasn't sure what to get you when I picked up my usual order."

The younger man stopped in the motion of picking out a book, returned to the chairs, and stared at Justin. He contemplated the cup carrier and pulled his eyebrows together under the brim of the fedora. "Pardon? You got me... What? Why?"

Justin placed one of the cups down and pulled a scone from the bag. He stuck it on a napkin and slid it across. "You look like you could use something warm in your belly. I chose hot chocolate with extra whip cream and fudge swirl on top and a blueberry scone from Starbucks. I didn't know if you'd prefer coffee or a latte. You come in every day and don't eat much other than a single thin sandwich. It must get a little boring to have the same thing and not much else."

"You don't know me."

"I was hoping we could change that too. Sit. Enjoy some breakfast." Justin sat in the other chair, opened the top to his vanilla soy latte, and blew away the rising steam. He sipped the fragrant coffee and sighed with pleasure. "Ahh, my caffeine nirvana delivered from heaven." Then he tugged out a holiday special apple pound cake and bit into one end of the sweet cinnamon, roasted apple, and delicious slice. "I've been waiting for this to come back around on the menu."

The young man settled the battered seabag and messenger bag on the floor next to his chair, tugged off the gloves and his coat. Losing the outer later revealed his slender, lanky frame dressed in a worn sweater, plaid shirt, and jeans ripped at one knee as he sat. He pulled off the black fedora, ran his fingers through the flattened golden hair to fluff the short spiky locks, and tossed the hat on top of the pile.

Justin smiled behind the cup. The hair looked softer today, but still the shaggy appearance of being self-cut. Somehow, the kid must have found a way to wash it along with the rest of him. He wondered how anyone could live in such a tenuous fashion. "Hey, this is a gorgeous hat. Very stylish," he said as he lifted the hat by the brim and checked it out.

"Thanks to a gift from a friend last December, I found it at a thrift store in a dollar bin. It's warmer than my old knit cap."

"Good find."

"Does the job." The kid shrugged as if he had nothing else to say. He wrapped both hands around the hot cup and sighed as the warmth invaded his fingertips. "Thanks for the cocoa. It's my favorite other than a cup of coffee macchiato, which is about as fancy as I get at one of those places. If I'm lucky, I grab a cup of the free coffee at the food store. Gotta time it right though." He took off the lid and sipped. He lifted his gaze over the cup and revealed unique grayish-blue eyes.

Those gorgeous eyes matched the golden spikes around the winsome face. Justin thought he'd just about died and gone to heaven as his cock thickened with delight. He wiggled his ass against the chair to rearrange his interested body.

"I'm glad I picked the right one." Justin paused for another long sip. "I prefer my vanilla soy latte."

"Soy?"

"Lactose intolerant," Justin explained.

"Ahh, must suck."

"Pain in the ass, but I deal with it. No indulging in a pint of Ben & Jerry's for me." Justin took another bite from the apple cake. "Who are you, my mystery reader? Can I at least have a name to go with those gorgeous eyes?"

The young man tucked his head down and flushed dark.

"Is there a problem with your name?"

"No, it's..." He fiddled with a bit of the scone. "Noel. My name is Noel Hudson."

"Noel?"

"Yeah, please don't break out in song or anything. I heard it all before."

"No problem here since my singing voice sucks big time. Guess you heard all the Christmas jokes?"

"Before I was five, I heard everything."

Justin chuckled.

"It sucks even more this time of the year." Noel rolled his eyes. "What makes things worse is I'm not into all the hoopla." He waved to the elegant decorations Justin placed with care and precision around the store. The rest of the town did the same level of decorations and more.

"Oh, that's too bad since it can be a wonderful warm holiday. Though, it's understandable if you had idiots annoying you all year round. I'm sure they were ten times worse when the holidays come around."

"Yeah, they never stopped."

"Are you a Christmas baby or is it a family name?"

"I was born this time of year." Noel bit into the scone. "This is delicious. Thanks."

"You're welcome. As I mentioned, I see you all day, but you nibble on one sandwich. That's not enough for someone your size. Hope you don't mind, but I've kept an eye on you the last few weeks."

"I need to watch my money." Noel bounced his knee several times. "Does it bother you if I sit here all day to read more than I could ever buy?"

"No, I don't mind. How did you find my store?"

"A nice cashier at a food store told me to look for this place when I asked about Blackbourne River."

"Really?"

"She comes here for the holidays to shop and loved it. I like books, so thought it would fit."

Justin leaned back as he sipped on his latte. "Don't you have anywhere else to be during the holidays?"

"Not at the moment, and the holidays are just another day to me. I never got into them, even as a kid."

"May I ask how you got in this situation?"

"Situation?" Noel tilted his head. Then he let out a soft sigh and shake of his head. "Are you trying to ask if I'm homeless?"

Justin pointed his hand at the battered bags on the floor. "It appears to me you're traveling with all of your possessions every day. It's not something to be ashamed of, not at all. Things are a little hard out there for everyone. One missed paycheck and someone else could lose everything."

Noel stared at him.

"Tell me about it."

"About what?"

"About what happened to bring you to this point of your life?"

"I was doing fine for years, managed to keep up with rent, bills, and food on a couple of lousy jobs. Struggling, but I had what I needed. I got sick with pneumonia and it screwed up the balance of everything. The doctors kept me in the hospital for weeks. When I got out, I didn't have a job."

"Damn, sorry that happened."

"They were two minimum-jobs at big warehouse type stores, but it kept me in a place and food." Noel shrugged, almost noncommittal as if nothing bothered him.

"When did this happen?"

"Four years ago."

Justin barely stopped his jaw from dropping at the quiet, matter-of-fact answer instead of a life-altering moment. "Have you been... homeless since?"

Noel nodded.

"It must be a struggle."

"You learn to adapt."

"What have you been doing since then?"

"Mostly, I figure out how to survive every day, find some food, some water, and figure out a place to spend the day. I hid out at a library to read and get on the computer while I lived in Boston. When I ran into another bout of trouble that put me back in the hospital, a couple of friends offered to give me another chance away from the city. They put me on a bus to Baltimore to stay with one of their friends while I get back on my feet."

"This isn't Baltimore."

"No, due to a stupid mistake and a twist of the world kicking my ass, I got left behind at the Wilmington station."

"Couldn't you call them back?"

Noel shook his head. "No. Too much guilt inside me."

"Why not? They would want to know."

"No. I couldn't let them know I screwed up again."

"Why?"

Closing his eyes, Noel let out a breath again. He opened his eyes and stared at his hands. "They did so much. I messed up, so I had to fix it. I wandered around on my way to Blackbourne, found a couple of cash paying jobs and places to sleep." He pulled off another piece of the scone and placed it in his mouth. Then he followed it with another sip of the hot chocolate.

"Did you walk here from Wilmington?"

"Yeah, it's not a bad walk. Pretty country if you stick by the river. As usual, things have been rough, but I survive."

There was that word again from him. Survive. Justin wondered if Noel knew about a life beyond simple survival. "Have things gotten worse?"

Noel tilted one shoulder in a half-shrug. "There's no bad or good in my situation. It's been better since I left Boston due to the rougher neighborhoods and competition for the good spots. Down here, I can wander a little more, but it's still just about survival. Weather is about the same."

"Do you have any help from your family?"

"Don't have any family."

"None at all?"

"Nope."

"It must be rough for you not to have any family. No one should be alone this time of the year."

"Wouldn't know what it was like to have a family to understand what it would be to miss them in my life," Noel said with a shrug. He plucked another piece from the scone as if he tried to make it last. "Things like that don't matter to me. I've always been alone since the moment I was born. As I said, I don't celebrate the holidays. At all."

"Excuse me?" This wasn't something he'd expected to find out when he'd started this conversation. There was something more to this young man. Now there was no way he could let Noel leave this store without his help. No one should be alone in the snow. "You haven't had anyone since you were born. What does that mean? Talk to me, please, perhaps I can help you if I know your story. The lady told you to come here for a reason. Right?"

Noel let out another sigh as if he was tired of talking. Then he met Justin's gaze. "I'm known as a safe-haven baby. Have you heard about the law?"

"I know it's a law to protect newborn babies from being abandoned in an unsafe location or the mother fearing prosecution. The mother is supposed to drop the baby at a hospital, fire station, or police station."

"That's the basic idea of it. My teen mom left me at a hospital in Boston. She passed me off to a nurse, said I was born in the morning on the twenty-third and left without giving her name. I wasn't even a day old when she left me helpless to the world. In accordance with the safe-haven infant law, no one could ask her anything else. The nurse named me Noel due to the holiday and Hudson, which was where she lived, and sent me to the newborn nursery to be checked out by the doctors."

Justin munched on another piece of the apple cake. "Wait, the nurse named you."

"They needed something for the paperwork. She gave me the name."

"Weren't you adopted? I thought newborns were always high on adoption requests." As one of three children of a wealthy family with a well-known name in DC, Justin had no idea what it was like to walk around with a name given to you based on a season and street. He couldn't imagine how lonely Noel must feel.

"Almost happened a couple of times, but something stopped things from being finalized. I phased out of the system seven years ago."

After a quick calculation in his head, Justin chewed on another piece. "You will be twenty-five this birthday. You don't look that old, I thought you were a teenager on the street."

"Doesn't matter what age I am. I don't bother celebrating a birthday. Why should I? No one cared when I came crying into the world, I was another folder on someone's desk. It's another day to survive to me since my mother didn't give a shit about me." Noel played with the rip on his knee.

"Hey there, now, you shouldn't say a thing—"

"Don't try to make anything nice about it. My teen mom, if one can call her that, dropped me off because she didn't want me for whatever reason. Perhaps she didn't want her parents or boyfriend to know she was pregnant and mess up the holidays with the family. The doctors figured she hid her pregnancy because I was scrawny and underweight. She didn't want to show a belly, so she starved herself and, in turn, me. What kind of mom does that to her child unless she's hiding something? If it wasn't for the law, she might have killed me."

Justin cursed under his breath. "Do you know why no one adopted you as a newborn?"

"Other than being underweight, no one wanted a baby with juvenile Type-1 diabetes. They don't want the broken ones."

"Do you require insulin? I mean, do you need to test on a regular basis and regulate your sugars with a meter thing?"

"Yup, the needles, strips, meter, and everything. The doctors found out when they checked me out, figured one of my teenage parents was diabetic, and I inherited the condition."

"Do you have your insulin?"

"Yeah, I have supplies."

"But it probably doesn't do much if you don't eat in a proper fashion to control your diabetes."

"Don't have much choice."

"What do you mean?"

"I don't have money to do everything I need. Because I was a ward of Massachusetts, I qualified for free medical. I have no records down here, so I get nothing. Before I left Boston, my nurse friend gave me a decent amount to survive until I found a new clinic in Baltimore, but I never made it there. I have some left, because I've been stretching out what I need."

"That is damn dangerous for your health."

"No other choice. I'm up and walking."

Justin rubbed a hand over his face and groaned. "Okay. This situation of yours is getting worse by the second."

"It's my life. I survive."

"Again with that word."

"What word?"

"Survive. It's all you say to describe your life."

Noel shrugged as if it didn't mean anything. "There's nothing else to say about it."

Justin glanced at the two battered bags and remembered how Noel hung out at the store all day. "Could I ask a few more questions?"

"Why not?" Noel stared back into the cup as if all the answers swirled within the dark chocolate brew. "I might as well get it all out."

"Thanks for trusting me."

"Don't have anything better to do."

Figuring he could deal with the sarcasm later and Noel deserved to be bitter after dealing with all this shit, Justin took another sip of the latte. "What other plans do you have? How are you planning on weathering the winter?"

Noel turned and glanced out the front window. "If a snowstorm blows through, maybe I could make some money shoveling driveways or sidewalk. Still need to figure out some plans on where to live. I haven't seen many condemned buildings I can get into for the night. A tent isn't going to do me much good in the snow. Is there a cheap motel somewhere?"

"Did you say a tent?" Justin held up a hand. "Back up four years ago again, I thought of something. Why didn't you get benefits back in Boston after losing your jobs?"

"Minimum wage and I wasn't at either place long enough. I had two jobs and worked shifts at both places to make enough money, because neither one hired full-time."

"No, no, you should have gotten them."

"Didn't. Doesn't matter anyway."

Justin rubbed his fingers against his temple. "Where are you living? In this tent?"

Noel swallowed hard and played with the cup.

"Noel, look at me, please. I need you to tell me the truth."

Noel lifted his worried gaze.

"I'm not going to turn you into the police or anything. Where are you living?"

"In my tent in the forest."

"The historical park."

"Yeah. I'm safest there than near the town where someone could find me. There's more shelter and safety in the forest."

"What about a bathroom? Shower?"

"I slip into the back of a local gym and used the showers. Rest of the stuff, I'm a nature boy."

"Another personal question here."

"Not like we haven't delved there."

"Are you gay?"

Looking up from the hot chocolate, Noel blanched.

Taking a chance, Justin leaned over and reached out to rest his fingers on Noel's bouncing knee to calm him. "It's okay. It isn't a problem or issue with me."

"Why do you ask?"

"I'm gay. I'm getting the sense that you are too," Justin said with a lopsided grin.

"Oh. Good. Your gaydar works fine." Noel bounced his knee harder, the force of it knocked Justin's touch from the faded jeans.

"Why don't you go to the local LGBT shelter?"

"I checked it out. They're full up and I'm too old. It's for teens."

"There should be one for young adults."

"Nope, I checked on my way here. Nothing. Wouldn't be the first time. Wouldn't be the last."

"Are you okay in your tent?"

"I manage. It's quiet. Don't have to worry about anyone bothering me. It's cold, but I learned to stuff crumpled newspaper inside the outer layer for additional insulation. Sometimes the simplest solutions work the best."

"Okay." Justin thought about the oversight and the possible problems. He filed it away as a future project to look into. "What happened during the winter when you were in Boston?"

"More shelters open up during the winter. If I was lucky to get a bed, I tried to keep it by offering to work around the shelter since they always need volunteers. During the warmer months, things are limited. Even if you were standing in line, you weren't guaranteed a spot."

"Do you stay here all day to get out of the cold?"

"There aren't many options. I have nowhere else to go, other than the library or the mall, but that's a walk back toward the city. The cold tires me out and if I burn more energy, I need food and insulin."

"Which is why you come here?"

"Your store is nicer than most of the other places. You don't kick me out like other owners nor do you play the annoying Christmas music all the time."

"I find a little variety in music brings customers in and gives them serenity from the season and stress." Justin looked around the shop. "What do you think about my shop? Do you like it? I know you like to read, but what else draws you here?"

"Yeah. It has a good feeling to the place. Kinda like you can curl up in a comfy chair and read all day as if you were home. You can never go wrong with a book. Just beyond every cover lies a brand new story only your mind can help to unlock." Some of Noel's fingers curled around the edge of the book. Then he stroke his fingers along the edges as if needing the tactile sensation to ground him. "I like getting lost in those worlds."

Justin smiled as Noel's gaze turned a little dreamy while he spoke about reading. "That's what I wanted to hear. We're going to change things around for you."

"Huh? Why?"

"Finish your breakfast and we'll get busy. Do you have your testing supplies and insulin?"

Noel dug his fingertips into the leather of the seat. "I keep everything in my bag. Why?"

"I didn't know about your diabetes and gave you a lot of sugar." Justin waved his hand toward the devoured scone and cocoa. "I want to make sure you test and balance the intake."

"Why do you ask though? I'm not a baby. I know how to handle my illness even during my current situation. I'm not trying to put myself into a coma or something."

"I know, but I need to learn."

"Why?"

Justin kept the grin at all the childish "Why" questions fired back at him. He wondered if Noel used them as a deflection from the truth or hiding something. "You'll find out in a minute." He waved his hand. "Go and test. I don't want to take the chance of you crashing. Once you're done, you can clean up and change into work clothes. We'll find a place to stash your bags for the day."

Noel tilted his head to the side. "What are you talking about? I'm not following you at all."

"Would you like a job?"

Noel blinked. "Why me?"

"You love books. You like my store. You need a chance. Everything I look for in a potential employee."

"Are you truly offering me a job?"

"Yes, if you would like a job. Here. With me at the shop."

A small, gentle smile curled Noel's lips. He nodded. "Yeah, I'll take it."

"Then it's done. You have a job. I need you to get into some work clothes. Do you have clean pants, a nice sweater, button down shirt and a different pair of shoes? I have a business casual policy along with the store's work vest."

Noel looked at his bags and shook his head. "No, no I don't. Everything is worn and dirty. It was clean when I left Boston, but since then..." He shrugged.

"That's understandable." Justin checked out Noel from head to toe. "Okay. We can fix all of this with ease. It isn't a problem."

"Of course it's a problem. Everything is torn and nasty."

Justin reached into his bag and pulled out a pad and pen. He pushed both across the table. "Write down your sizes in everything from underwear on up. I'll pick up some new clothes for the week. Consider them half of your first week's pay." He wouldn't bother deducting anything from the kid's pay, but he wouldn't tell Noel. Thanks to his grandparents, he had more than enough from his trust funds and could handle caring for one safe-haven baby who needed a helping hand and a decent break to get his bearings underneath him.

Noel glanced at him, lifted an eyebrow in a wary fashion. "What are you talking about?"

"Did I go to fast for you?"

Noel swooshed a hand over his head.

Justin chuckled at the motion. He figured he wouldn't get an easy acceptance about anything he offered to Noel. He didn't blame him. After being on the streets for so long, Noel would've lost trust and belief in most folks. It would take a while for Justin to earn Noel's trust that he wouldn't toss him aside. "Okay. We'll go through this again."

"A little slower."

He would need to be careful around Noel, not to push him too far and lose whatever momentum they built together. Part of his mind started to click with a wonderful, if crazy, plan he wanted to enact with this kid, who'd had such a rough life. He would play Secret Santa this year for an incredibly special person. It would be a special type of Secret Santa game.

"Well?" Noel held out his hands. "What's the deal?"

"I'm offering you a job. Here."

"Got that part. What's the job?"

"You're going to work here at BookWorm as another sales associate. Amy quit yesterday and I'm going crazy with the holiday hours. We have seven shopping days left in this season and I need to make them count. You know the store since you've been here every day and pretty much been to every corner of it. I'll show you how to handle the inventory, clean, shelve, and pull books for online orders."

"Just like that you're giving me this job, on the spot. Why? You know nothing about me."

"Thanks to this chat and how you opened up to me, I believe I know you a little better than you think. You'll get twelve bucks an hour to start plus overtime."

"What? Twelve dollars an hour? That's above minimum."

"I always pay above minimum. You're saving me from going crazy. One of my clerks quit during the craziest time of the year and she damn well knew it. Like I said earlier. You love books. You need a job. It's a win-win situation for both of us."

"I don't..."

"Accept the offer, please, Noel. I'm not going to accept a refusal."

"Okay. Okay. I accept the position."

"Excellent."

Noel cleared his throat and rubbed his hands together. "Thank you."

"More than welcome," Justin said with a warm smile. "We're happy to have you onboard. We'll fill out paperwork later." He finished his latte and the last of the apple cake. "Dang, love this stuff, I should have gotten another one."

"What do you want me to do?"

"Oh. Sorry. Sorry. This cake is one of my holiday vices." Justin wiped his fingers on a napkin to clean them. "I need you to write down your sizes so I can go shopping." He would gather a few more things to put his Secret Santa plan in action, but he had to take care and not frighten him. Though Noel put up a damn punchy front, underneath there was a scared rabbit. No matter what, this was going to be the best holiday season ever.

"I can't believe this." Noel scribbled down what Justin wanted. "Why are you doing this for me? Even with a chat, you still don't know me from the next guy on the street. And I come from the streets, so I know what is out there."

"You've come in here every day for two weeks solid. You're quiet and conscientious of others around you. You're an honest fella who hasn't had the best path in life." Justin leaned forward and placed his hand on Noel's knee. "I didn't want to see you standing out in the damn snow every day and hiding from the world in my store. I wondered who you were and where you would go once I closed the store. My grandparents taught me over years not to ignore anyone, but to do something to change what I believe is wrong. I think your situation fits the bill."

Noel stared down and then up at Justin. "Man, I could be a total loser giving you a sob story to steal everything from you."

"I'll be blunt." Justin captured Noel's gaze with his direct one. "Are you conning me?"

Noel blanched.

Justin lifted his hand and pointed a finger at him. "I didn't think so. It isn't in you."

"How..."

"Good judge of character. This conversation cemented my decision along with your behavior these last couple of weeks. Every day, you select a book to read and you put it back on the shelf. I even see you fixing things on the shelf. You're not a thief or trying to scam me, Noel." Justin dropped his hand again on Noel's knee. "I have a guest room at home too. You're welcome to stay there. No more about this sleeping in a tent thing, it's ridiculous to think about it. There's been talk about a dangerous cold front heading our way. You can't stay out in the forest."

"Really? You're not going to expect anything from me? I mean—"

"What? Oh!" Justin reddened, shook his head, dropped his hand from Noel's knee, and cleared his throat. "No, no, no." He waved his hand. "I don't expect you in my bed in exchange for anything I'm doing to help you. If you want me, hell, it is your choice all the way. Though on my end, you're adorable and way cute. So, yeah, I want you, but I won't take advantage of the situation."

Noel flushed fifty shades of red.

"Noel?"

"WoulditbesobadifIwantedtobeinyourbed?" he muttered all in one word.

Justin cocked his head to the side. Did he hear Noel say what he thought he did? Perhaps his Secret Santa plan could work after all. He hoped it wouldn't scare Noel away. No matter what, he had to offer him the safe haven he seemed to crave. This beautiful young man needed to have those shadows removed from his gorgeous grayish-blue eyes, the exhaustion banished from the slender shoulders, a full belly of good food, clean warm clothes on his slim frame, and a soft pillow where he could sleep without being on guard. Hopefully, along with all the friendship, light, and warmth Justin could pour back into his heart. Not to mention, Justin wanted to show Noel there was more to a birthday and Christmas than loss and heartache. He would figure out all the details as he pulled this cockamamie plan together. He might scramble a couple of days, but it would come together. Either way, there were eight days to Christmas, so he had to make it work.

Swallowing hard, still bright red, Noel tucked his head down. "I gotta go test and wash up like you said. Here's the stuff you asked for." He grabbed both of his bags, scrambled to his feet, and raced off to the bathroom.

Justin chuckled as he took the pad. "I'm going to lock you in the store and be back in about a half hour," he yelled as he ripped off the top sheet.

"Okay," Noel called back, his voice muffled by the door.

After he wound his scarf around his neck, Justin pulled on his coat, checked to see if his wallet was in the inner pocket, then tucked the piece of paper with it, and zipped and buttoned. He locked the door, walked down to a clothing store, and slipped inside against the cold wind. He waved to the owner, a good friend, pulled out the list, and went shopping. This wouldn't be the first store he stopped in to enact his super-secret plan to give Noel the best Christmas ever.

Chapter Three

Hours later, dressed in soft khakis, a navy button-down shirt, and a steel gray sweater with comfortable gray sneakers, Noel couldn't believe how his rotten luck changed in the course of a couple of hours. Not what he expected after waking up in his tent this morning. Now he wore a simple blue vest with the store's logo stitched across the back to signify his status as an employee.

It looked like the lady back at the Wilmington food store was right. This place was rather... well... magical.

In a matter of a morning, he went from standing in the freezing cold to working in one of his favorite stores. This place was even better than the library because there was an entire section of LGBTQ+ and yaoi books he wanted to dive into once he finished the *Dark Hunters* and the other connected series. He gathered another stack of books from the cart he alphabetized earlier. He sorted each group within their genre and place on the shelves.

All this bounty came from the good graces of his crush — the hottest man he'd laid eyes on in the longest time. A man with one of the kindest hearts, but not to the point where he let someone walk all over him.

Justin offered his help and support, but Noel needed to work and prove himself. He couldn't lie around, do nothing, and expect everything handed over to him. He knew others who tried to pull that stuff and he hated them and their weakness and greed. He swore he would never turn into one of them, but it had been so hard to get back on his feet after four years of going nowhere. Sarah and Lenora were right; he needed a complete change of his outlook on life and his location to get there. Perhaps Justin could show him the way.

"Hey there, you've been busy. How's the shelving going?" Justin wandered around, one hand in his pocket. He wore the same vest as Noel, not keeping himself apart from his employees.

"Good. I'm almost finished with the shipment." Noel waved a hand at the cart. He'd emptied all but the top tier.

"Damn, you did a helluva lot better job than Amy and Joe. They whine like babies whenever we get a shipment. Usually took them at least two days to empty a full shipment," Justin said. "Should have known something was up with them." He slid fingers through the brunet sweep of hair that covered the right side of his face with the same elegance as the rest of his movements, pushing it back, but most of it fell forward again.

"I don't know why anyone would complain. This isn't a hard or complicated job. It's opening boxes, check their tags, sort in their genres, alphabetize them, and put them out. If you get some extra time, you can check out the blurbs to see what's interesting." Noel shrugged while he rearranged a shelf and lifted the four new books into place, arranging the covers out to display them. He remembered seeing the young pair of lovers. They'd stood together in the far corner, kissing and flirting. He wasn't surprised they complained to Justin, who was such an easygoing boss. "I like working back here amongst the shelves and books. I hope you don't mind, but I helped a bunch of customers too. I offered them suggestions for gifts and such and showed them where to find the books."

"Mind? Heck no, that is all part of the job. One of the reasons I snuck back here to find you. They told me the new guy gave them a bunch of help to find the ideal gift, which is awesome news for you. It's what I want to hear," Justin said with a big grin and a sparkle in his pine-green eyes. "I told you how you were precisely what we need around here."

Noel ducked his head and flushed. "I enjoy books."

"Same here for me. It's the reason why I ended up owning this place instead of being stuck in a boring financial office." Justin caressed the spines of books and glanced to Noel with a soft smile.

"You said your family was from DC. How did you come to be here?"

"I spent a lot of my childhood here with my maternal grandparents. They owned a home here. I had trouble at the private school my parents insisted I attend. Even as a boy, I was a bit...flamboyant. It didn't go down well in a strict private school."

"Catholic?"

"No. Privileged. I wanted nothing to do with those small-minded idiots who only cared about status, clothes, and other prissy shit. I stayed true to me and was bullied ridiculously for it. At her wit's end, my mother shipped me here to her mother. Grandma enrolled me in the public school and I never left."

"Why didn't you go back to your parents?"

"They had my other siblings to groom and polish. I was nothing like them. I belonged here, like I belong in this little store." Justin tilted his head as the smile grew. "I saw the same love in your eyes and the way you handle the books and customers. You pass on the same joy of reading. You're a good match here. A clerk in a bookstore may not seem like a big shot, but we open new worlds, and help those who are learning to read a way to climb out of their dark places into a better one." He picked up books from the back end of the cart, checked the author, and moved down the aisle. With grace and ease, he shifted and moved books to set the new ones in place. "By the way, William came in to help cover the front. We're going to order in lunch from the deli down the street. The menu is at the front. Let's go pick out a sandwich and drink. You can return and finish this."

"Should I leave the cart here?"

Justin nodded.

Noel shoved his hands in pockets and stepped around the cart. "I don't have..."

"Don't start about money. The shop covers meals during this crazy season. My rules. I'm the boss and I like to do things differently for my employees. I'll be taking care of you until we get you back on your feet," Justin said as he slung an arm around Noel's shoulders. "We need to get you back on a healthy diet with your diabetes. I'm worried about you. I know you want to feel independent again, but I want you to cooperate and work with me without arguing about everything."

"I'm okay," Noel protested.

"No, you look tired and underfed. Unhealthy in my eyes," Justin said, "and don't even try to tell me you're fine."

"Why do you ask?"

"I didn't. I'm only saying you need to get healthy."

Noel rolled his eyes in an exasperated fashion.

Justin leaned back and stared at him. "You're a good fifty or more pounds underweight, malnourished, and who knows what is going on with your diabetes. We should get you in to a doctor too."

"I don't have insurance."

Justin waved a hand to dismiss the issue. "I'll figure out a way to add you to the store's coverage for the other associates." He smiled at a customer, who greeted them as they passed.

They went around the back of the large front desk where an older man with receding silver gray hair and wire-rimmed glasses sat on a stool by the computer. He finished checking out a mother and son, bagged a pile of books in a colorful BookWorm canvas bag, and handed the receipt to the lady. "Have a wonderful holiday and thanks for shopping at BookWorm. Happy reading!"

"Merry Christmas!" the lady said. "Bye, Justin!"

"Bye, Mrs. Grant, I'll see you both at the party this weekend," Justin said with a wave.

"We would never miss it. Sunday evening?"

"Right. Starts at four, my place as usual," Justin said. "Bye, Andy, I hope Santa is good to you."

"Bye-bye, Mr. Justin and Mr. New Guy," the five-year-old said with a wave of his mitten-covered hand and walked out with his mom.

Noel chuckled and waved at the kid. He looked to Justin. "Party?"

"I throw a party for Addicts and all staff at my place the Sunday before Christmas. It's a tradition." Justin turned to William. "I would like to introduce you to our mystery reader and new employee, Noel Hudson. I hired him this morning after a long chitchat since Amy quit last night and eloped with Joe, who quit on my voicemail. Idiot didn't have the balls to say it to my face." Justin rolled his eyes.

William dropped his mouth in shock. "They didn't!"

Noel looked between them. "I often saw them kissing and flirting in the far back corner."

"Really? During business hours." Justin shoved a hand through his hair and grumbled when Noel bobbed his head. "Unbelievable. Real nice. I tolerate a lot, but that..." He let out a long snort of disgust. "I don't know why I kept them around for as long as I did."

"You're too damn soft-hearted," William said.

"I know. I know." Justin leaned his head back to study the cameras above them. "Looks like I need to fix those camera positions to cover the corners."

"Perhaps add another one to fix the blind spot."

"Ugh, I hate adding security. Nice of them, huh? It's not real smart, if you asked me. I don't plan on accepting either one back as employees. The idiots left us in a lurch. Because they quit, I legally don't have to offer them unemployment," Justin said as he leaned a hip against the counter.

Since he knew what it meant not to have a steady paycheck in his pocket, Noel had no idea why someone would deliberately cut themselves off. "What were they thinking?"

"Not with their brains, kid," William said with a snort. He stuck out his hand. "William Bonnaire. It's nice to meet you, son."

Noel shook hands and said, "Same here, sir."

"Just William will do. I'm not a Bill or Billy or Will. I'm a full on William."

"Gotcha. I'm stuck with Noel. Simple and pronounced like the 'nole in Seminole not No-elle. No singing carols to me."

"You don't want to hear this singing voice any more than the kid's here," William said with a smile and nod toward Justin.

"Phew!" Noel wiped a hand over his forehead in a playful sarcastic fashion. "I'm safe from the annoyance then."

Justin bumped Noel's shoulder with his and grinned. "Pass over the deli menu and let Noel take a look. Call in an order when Noel makes his decision, William, and set it for delivery. Use the company account as usual. I'll have my usual rustic ham on wheat, a cup of lemony orzo soup with a sweet tea," he said.

"Right, boss," William said while he jotted down Justin's order on a pad.

Noel noticed Justin's roll of the eyes at William calling him "boss" and wondered if there was an inside joke.

William winked at Noel and passed over the folded menu. "Here you go, young fella. Anything you want. They make great soups, paninis, and sandwiches. All fresh."

When he glanced around at hearing a soft noise, Noel looked around the store.

A woman approached from the stacks with a flustered expression upon her face. She thumbed the screen on her iPhone. "Coffee table book. Architecture. Really?" She stood next to Justin. "Excuse me, I'm sorry to bother you."

Since he heard the same thing, Justin turned with a friendly smile. "Not a problem. I'm Justin, how can I help?"

"I need help. Oh, sorry, Patti," she said.

Justin chuckled. "It's okay. What are you looking for?"

"I need to find a coffee table book. Something with architecture, if you have anything."

"We have a splendid selection of fabulous coffee table books. I'm sure there's something about architecture. I think there is a new one about New York. Let me show them to you."

"Oh, thank you. I don't know a thing about architecture, but my best guy pal is one. I thought I would get something in his field. He adores New York. A book from there would make my day and a dead-on gift." She thumbed the screen to double-check something. "Yes, those are my notes on the list for Kayden—coffee table book, architecture, and New York. He prefers cityscapes."

Noel watched Justin listen patiently as Patti prattled on while they moved through the store. "He's damn good at his job, isn't he," he said, not asking or expecting an answer.

"Yup, he's been here since he was a teenager in high school and owns the whole place. You wouldn't guess from looking at him, but the boy came from one of the most prominent families of Blackbourne River."

"I thought his family was in DC."

"That's his father's family. They're all senators and stuff. His mother's family is from here, the Blackbournes of Blackbourne River."

"Are you kidding?"

William shook his head.

Noel glanced at the stacks and back to William. "Is Justin rich?"

"Was rich, he doesn't consider himself anymore."

"How can you no longer be rich?"

"His parents dropped him, in a fashion, when he left that fancy-dancy private school and turned down working for his father in either the family business or the Capitol. He stayed here at the store."

"Why would someone do that to him?"

"Yeah, they're such nice family, huh?" William snorted. "Even with money, family isn't perfect, kid."

"Why would his parents turn Justin away? He's been nothing but warm-hearted and giving to me. Is it because he's gay?"

"No, they didn't have a problem with him coming out. It's a funny situation. When he came out to them, the news rolled right over them. I think because Justin is a second son and his older brother was already married and his wife pregnant."

"So they didn't care if Justin couldn't carry on the family names."

"Who knows with those folks? Luckily, he and his maternal grandparents were tight and loving. When they passed, they made sure to put the bulk of the inheritance in a trust for Justin to see him through his life. His parents were pissed, especially his mother since she got a pittance from them, and tried to fight it, but the will was ironclad and remained in Justin's favor."

"Good for him to have a back-up."

"He doesn't really use it."

"Did they cast him out for working at a bookstore?"

"No, because he chose a simple store instead of his father's more prestigious financial firm or even higher up the hill on the Capitol. They couldn't believe anyone would turn down a chance to work on the Capitol. They believe he's underutilizing his degree and education. I call bullshit on all their complaints," William said, tapping his finger against the counter. "Justin's drive and love of the business is one of the few reasons why the BookWorm is still here. He competes against the big names and Internet craziness. Though, Justin knew when to build a website and offer books on the Internet for customers who want the same experience they get by walking in the doors. He gets on a chat if they request one-on-one help. If they can't find a particular book, he'll go out and find the book, buy it, and sell it to them. In the last couple of years, he signed on to have the ability to become an e-book seller. Either at the laptop station set up by the window or the wall of postcards next to it. Each card has a download code. Once they purchase it, the system activates the code. They go home, either scan or type in the code, and it appears in their e-reader."

Noel lifted an eyebrow. "He does all that?"

"He'll do whatever he can and more. He goes to estate sales, auctions, antique stores, flea markets, and anywhere else to find books. Sometimes he makes rare finds and brings them back. We don't only offer new books, but used and rare ones too. Most of the rare ones are kept under lock and key in those protective glass cabinets or in the back room under careful atmospheric conditions to protect them. People bring in gently used ones for a store discount, which we keep track of in our system. You'll see those books stamped with our logo," William said.

"Those are the books in the back corner?"

"That's right."

"Wow, it must help out a lot of people."

"He's always done it. Even before the economy got bad, he looked beyond the next year to keep ahead. He'll allow some folks to borrow books like a library and either they can return them or purchase the book." William nodded to get Noel to turn around. "There we go, less than five minutes, and we have a sale."

Noel watched Justin reappear with Patti, who clutched a large coffee table book in her hands. They continued their discussion, only the flustered look was gone.

"Thank you so much, Justin. Kayden is going to love it," she said.

"This one came out a few months ago. It's a little different from standard architecture since it's about the rooftop gardens of New York City, but I think he's going to enjoy the scenery and design. If there is any problem, please feel free to bring the book back and we can help him exchange it for something else that he discovers on the shelves," Justin said. "William can ring you up, Patti. Have a wonderful Christmas and please come on back to BookWorm anytime."

"Oh, after this, you better believe I will." Patti danced over to the register with the book and two others. "I couldn't resist picking these up while I was here for me to enjoy. I need something to help me relax during this crazy season." She laughed while pulling out her wallet.

"Don't I know it," William agreed while ringing her up. "Are you a BookWorm Addict?"

"What's that?"

William explained to her about the special program that was called the Addict club that included a low annual membership price that included discounts, special offers, and unique get-togethers or signings. His explanation intrigued Noel.

With another laugh, she waved her hand. "What the hell... Sign me up. After this, I'll be back. I'm usually an e-book reader, but there's something about holding a book in your hands."

"I know how you feel, but we also sell e-books here if you ever have questions about a book. I'll add the information to the bag so you can look it over," William said. "Okay. Just need a few details for you to fill out on this little pad and you're an Addict." He took her through the simple process as she tapped the stylus on the screen. "I'll add the membership fee to your purchase."

"Make your lunch decision." Justin sidled next to Noel and tapped a finger on the menu.

Tugging the menu closer, Noel perused it. "How did you know about the architecture book?"

Justin polished his fingers in a teasing fashion on his shirt. "I'm a book genius..."

Noel punched his shoulder.

"Hey." Justin grinned. "I know my stock and I fixed the area yesterday before I left. I discovered the book then and flipped through the pages after the cover caught my attention. Memory is pretty decent," he admitted. "You'll get the hang of it, especially for certain sections of the store."

"By the way, William's good at finishing the sale," Noel murmured.

"William was the previous owner and taught me everything when I found the place as a kid. In high school, I worked here whenever I could. William had a series of heart attacks and out of the blue he offered me the store for a small price."

"Really? He told me about your family. The parts you didn't bother to mention."

Justin grimaced. "Surprised the living hell out of me, but I didn't want to see this old place go to some stranger who wouldn't understand the history or might make it disappear. I knew what BookWorm meant to the community. They would have gutted it and turned it into something boring, like another fancy-dancy gallery or chotskies shop." He looked around at what he saved. "I wanted nothing to do with my father's boring business or those blasted white marble buildings. My grandparents supported my decision before they passed and I follow their judgment and advice more than my parents."

"What did you figure out with the store?"

"This happened before the e-book craze started, so physical books were the only option. I did my research. The nearest bookstore was in the mall, which as you know is closer to Wilmington than here, so I had a steady stream of customers and could build from there. William had a lot of loyal customers who came here for every book they purchase. I wouldn't lose them. I managed to work out a decent proposal, finances, got a small loan, and showed what I created to William and the bank."

Intrigued by the story, Noel leaned closer and listened. "What happened?"

"William cracked up with laughter, impressed by all the steps I took at his simple question. He knew I wasn't an idiotic fool like his two sons, who could care less about his pride and joy, and his store would be in good hands. I mentioned my one small counter-offer. I wanted him to stay with me and the store, but part-time. He could help during the holiday season because this is his favorite time of year, and weekends when he feels strong. No matter what happens, I can count on him for anything. The rest of the year, he stays retired and dabbles in his gardening and hobbies."

"Is that why you roll your eyes whenever he calls you boss?"

"He does it to tease me, since he's been my boss a whole lot longer than I've been his. He can be a crazy old man."

"But he's a special one to you."

"My father could care less about me and my maternal grandfather passed before I started high school. I floundered for a bit. William entered into the role of father, far warmer and kinder than mine. My grandma always said kind things about him and this store. She talked William into letting me work part-time during school when I got old enough. I'm not saying I ever knew what it was like to be without a family. I had a family, but not the traditional kind. Not since I left that horrendous private school and came here." Justin cleared his throat and tapped his finger on the menu. "Sorry, I didn't mean to bring up the past. Choose something so we can order."

"I don't mind talking about it. Oh, yeah, food is good. You're right, this is an interesting menu." Noel opened it to study the choices again. "I'll have the sun-dried pesto chicken panini with an iced tea."

"That's delicious, you're gonna love it. Want a cup of soup? It's damn cold out today."

"No, this is good. Do they have the number of sugars and carbs on this?"

"I'll have William ask when he orders. Do you need to know?"

"The numbers helps to figure out my insulin shot."

"No problem." Justin jotted down Noel's order on William's pad and made a note about the sugars and carbs and circled it. "Want to share a large order of sweet potato fries?"

"Do they have them?"

"Yeah, they're delicious."

"Uhh, sure, I'll need to add those carbs in as well."

"No problem, and I'll see if William can get the carbs for everything on the menu so we don't have to ask every time." Justin added it to the order and another note. "They'll get it down here for us in a bit. William will cover for us and he'll eat after. You and I will finish our day around five, do your paperwork, and take off. My assistant manager, Jamie, scheduled himself for the three to close shifts for the week. William will help him."

"What about us?"

"You and I will handle the seven to five shifts. I'll figure out what we'll do for Christmas Eve according to the sales figures and demand. It's up to us four since the other two took off for wedded bliss." Justin grimaced at the words and shook his head. "I think the four of us should be able to handle everything on our own. If not, I'll put up a Help Wanted sign and see who answers it."

Noel snorted and chuckled. "Sorry." He broke off in laughter.

"I wish them the best, but horrid timing from a store owner's standpoint. So not going to send them a wedding gift." Justin joined him in laughter.

"What's wrong with you two?" William asked after he finished with Patti.

Justin wiped the tears from his eyes. "We're discussing scheduling and whatnot to balance out the four of us. The store remains closed from Christmas Eve to the twenty-seventh. Same thing for New Year's Eve, New Year's Day, and reopen on the third."

"Did you decide not to open on Christmas Eve?"

"Not sure yet, but if I open, I'll work a seven to twelve day. I'll check the bottom line and listen to the customers. If I hear the need for last-minute shopping, we can open for them. How does the rest sound to you?"

"Sounds fine to me, a nice break after all the craziness," William said.

"I'll put a help wanted sign out around the end of January to pick up one or two more associates to help us out."

"Is there enough demand for another clerk? If young Noel decides to stay with us, I'm sure we can handle things."

"I'm not going anywhere," Noel said.

"Good to hear. See? He's a young fella. He's strong."

"I'll think about it. Four of us mean longer shifts and I don't like having that. We'll see what happens." Justin pushed the orders to William. "Call those in to the deli. Ask about the sugars and carbs for the menu, will ya?"

"Sure. Any reason why?"

"I'm a diabetic," Noel said as he looked down at the counter.

"Understand. I can handle it. No problem, kiddo." William moved to the other end and dialed the number.

"I'm going to finish off the cart. Should I clear off the tables and shelve the books?" Noel asked as he pushed away.

Justin studied him. He gave him a lazy nod of acceptance.

Noel wandered away and disappeared back into the shelves. He kept half his mind on the gorgeous man, who'd saved him from the cold, snow, and his miserable life. His cock came to attention and he pressed the heel of his hand against his fly with a muttered curse.

"So not the time to get a damn boner," he told himself. "Not when it concerns my boss." He forced himself to return to work.

Chapter Four

After the delicious lunch, the rest of the afternoon flew. Helping customers, keeping the store tidy, gathering books for online orders to ship before the holiday, Noel lost count of how many times he circled the store. His feet ached, but unlike the days he walked around outside, this was the good kind. It was a well-spent day working on his feet. He kept busy until Justin ordered him to the back office.

"You called for me," Noel said as he leaned against the doorframe.

"Hey, there you are." Justin lifted his gaze from the crazy disorganized desk and grinned. "Go ahead and hang up the vest and grab your messenger bag. I have your seabag in the corner here. You're off the floor. We need to fill out your paperwork. I'll show you how to clock in and out, and we'll get out of here," Justin said while he waved to the chair.

Noel removed the vest and hung it on one of the pegs. He grabbed his messenger bag from the locker and returned to the office. He walked behind Justin's desk to grab the seabag and returned to sit in a chair.

"If you have them, I need to see two forms of ID. If not, we'll figure a way around it."

"Just an old Boston identity card since I never learned to drive." Noel tugged it out from his flat wallet and slid it over.

"We can work with this... Hold on—" Justin broke out in a yawn, stretched his arms high, and twisted his back until his spine cracked. "Ahh. Needed that, sorry. Long day as you know." He lowered his arms. "I need you to fill this section." He pushed a form across with a pen.

"Do you need another latte or regular coffee?"

"Oh, no, not this late, I'll never sleep. I'll hang in there for a few more hours to get us home."

"Home?"

"You and I are heading to my place after this. There's no wiggling out of this decision, buster." Justin pointed his pen at Noel.

Staying quiet about that part, Noel filled in his information. He noticed Justin stuck a post-it note with an address on the form. "What's this?" He flicked the edge.

"You're going to use my address for the forms."

"Really?"

"I'm too tired to argue with you about this." Justin dropped his head on the desk. "Noel, please, I'm not sending you back out in the snow. Write. I'm hungry and tired. Do you have any other things?"

Noel pulled in his lower lip.

Justin picked his head up a little and stared at Noel. "Please tell me you have more than what's stuffed in the seabag and what I purchased for you. I'm not interested in a late-night shopping trip."

"No, this is all I have. Everything I left Boston with is in these bags." Noel tapped the pen on the desk.

"You haven't been in our small town long."

"No, I arrived around December first and looked for a job, but nothing was available. I managed to get what little money I could and lived in my tent."

"Where were you before?" Justin waved a hand. "Wait... You mentioned a city earlier this morning, but I forgot the name." He snapped his fingers together a few times.

"You're tired."

"Brain dead. I get this way this time of the year. Helping people too many times, too many titles, too many authors... empties my brain. I'll recharge overnight, trust me."

"Boston, I came here from Boston."

"Holy crap! Did you walk all the way from Boston? Wait... you explained this too."

"I did. Partially. My friends gave me a bus ticket for Baltimore, but I lost my ride in Wilmington. I walked from there."

"Right. Right. I still can't believe you slept outside in the cold. Are you nuts?"

"The tent is old, but rated for the cold weather and waterproof, plus I layered my clothes. I know how to make a decent fire and catch a rabbit or hook a fish. I'm pretty handy to have around."

"Impressive." Justin shook his head. "I'm sorry you had to live in such a fashion."

"I knew no other way."

"Most would have given up in your position. Whined, complained, done something else, but you kept moving." Another yawn escaped Justin and he waved a hand in front of his face in apology. "Sorry, sorry. Don't mean to." He opened bottle of a bright red sports drink and gulped down a few swallows. "Ahh, yummy. Okay. So no other stops, that's good. Straight home we go." He tilted the bottle to Noel. "Do you want one? I keep a stash in here for emergencies."

Noel shook his head. He didn't bother to protest about going home with Justin, since he knew Justin would stop the words before they left his mouth. He scribbled in the rest of his information and signed his name. He pushed the papers back to Justin, who filled in his sections, signed, and handed the ID card back to Noel. Justin showed him how to sign into the computer, which Noel repeated and set his personal password. He wrote it down on a scrap piece of paper and stuck it in one of the messenger bag's pockets.

Justin logged them both out. "Got it?" He chugged another few swallows of the drink.

"Simple."

"Yup, I try to keep things easy. If you forget the password, I can reset it. Oh, those are your new clothes." Justin pointed to the three bags in a different corner than his seabag.

Noel twisted to see them, since he missed them earlier. "I thought you got me one..."

"Why? You would need to do laundry every night. Nah, would be stupid of me to do such a thing. Plus, I figured you would need underwear and socks. I bought enough for a week as I said I would."

"Justin..."

"What? Please accept. It's not charity or pity, I'm only trying to—"

Unable to stop himself, Noel threw his arms around Justin's shoulders, stopping him in mid-explanation. He pressed his face against Justin's neck.

"You'll be all right, sweet boy. Things will get better. I promise," Justin whispered as he enclosed Noel's thin frame in his warm embrace. "All you need to do is accept the help without fighting me every step. It's all I ask."

Noel remained quiet as he stayed in Justin's arms.

"Ssh. You're not alone. Not anymore," Justin whispered. He pressed his lips in a gentle kiss within Noel's hair and temple.

Noel's heart clenched with the simple, but so powerful words.

After another squeeze, Justin leaned back, cupped his hand around Noel's cheek. "Okay?"

Noel tilted his face against Justin's hand. "Yeah, I'll try not to fight or protest, but—"

"It's an automatic answer. I know."

"Give me time. Okay."

"All you want, sweet boy." Justin kissed his cheek again. "Change your sneakers for your other shoes. Probably should get you a decent pair of snow boots. More snow fell while we were busy. We need to leave, get your things, and go home before I fall asleep standing up. I'm ready to eat some dinner and relax. How about you?"

Stepping away, Noel shoved a hand through his hair and gathered his scattered emotions together. "Yeah, me too. A long hot shower or bath would be nice."

"Perhaps you should indulge in both."

Noel chuckled, knowing he was on the grimier side of things even after the quick showers in the gym.

"No offense."

"None taken. I know what I look like."

Justin hummed, but didn't say anything.

Noel placed his new sneakers back in their box and shoved his feet into his battered boots, which had so many miles under their soles. Along with several layers of duct tape in different sections. He noticed Justin did the same, stepping into the pair of sneakers he'd worn this morning. He slid the strap of his seabag over one shoulder, then the messenger bag across his body and picked up the shopping bags.

About twenty minutes later, Justin pulled his dune-colored Soul into the garage of a two-story home. He led Noel through the garage to the door.

"Home sweet home. Let me switch on the outside Christmas lights." Justin plugged in a bright orange plug. "There we go." He opened a door and led Noel into the granite and stainless-steel kitchen. "Let me show you where you'll be staying. There are three guest rooms down the hall from me. A den was down here and I turned it into an office. What was called a living room off the foyer is now a library." He moved them through a comfortable family room and turned up a single flight of stairs.

Noel followed as he looked around at the simple, clean furniture with a splash of bright accent colors and stylish decorations. Everything seemed to work together.

"Your home is great," he said.

"Thanks. A little eclectic, I know. I pick up pieces that talked to me, not necessarily a particular style per say."

"Never gave a thought to decorating anything since I didn't have the money for extra stuff when I worked."

Justin looked over his shoulder and down the upstairs hallway. He made a strange call with his mouth. "Hmm. Strange."

Noel lifted an eyebrow and peered around Justin. "What is strange?"

"Oh, I'm wondering where Marlowe and Raleigh got themselves to. They always greet me at the door, demanding their dinner and attention, but they didn't tonight. Perhaps they're upset I'm late." He made different chirping noises and calls.

"Who are Marlowe and Raleigh?"

"They're my silver short-haired Ragdoll cats, a pair of brothers I found in the local shelter. I named Marlowe after Christopher Marlowe, an Elizabethan—"

"He was a poet and playwright known for *Faustus*," Noel interrupted. "I assume Raleigh is named for Sir Walter Raleigh, an adventurer who fell for Bess, the lady in waiting to the queen."

"You know your history as well as literature."

With a shrug, Noel looked around for signs of the cats. "I enjoyed Elizabethan history, unlike others in my class, often used the time for my reports. I did the same with Shakespeare and Marlowe in English classes."

"Not many kids can say such a thing," Justin said.

"Yeah, an odd thing, but it lifted me out of my dreary life of different temporary homes I got shuffled too."

"I'm sure they're hiding, wondering who the stranger is in their home. Give them a few moments to collect your scent and vibe. They're friendly critters and will poke their noses out soon." He stopped at a door. "Back to decorating, I'm sure your home would be a reflection of you."

"I look forward to meeting them on their terms." After another look around the hallway, Noel played with the strap of his messenger bag. "There are times I'm not sure who I am, other than an orphan on the move, trying to keep his head above water."

"You'll figure yourself out. Take the time here and at the store to give yourself a chance to rest, heal, and figure out what you want. Things at the store quiet down a bit after the holidays. Like I mentioned, the workweek drops to Wednesdays through Sundays, so you'll have time to kill."

"Sounds like a good plan to me."

"Perhaps we could set you up with a college program, if you want. We have an awesome community college."

"I never had the grades or money to think about college."

Justin shrugged. "Thought I'd give you something else to think about while you figure out what you want. I want you to think about options and we'll discuss them as you want." He stopped at a door. "Here we go. This is the guest room."

Noel entered an inviting room filled with a full-size bed with a sunlit leaves patterned comforter in shades of gray set against a black frame with sleek matching furniture. He dropped his bags on the floor, noticed a gray area rug against the wooden floor. In the corner, Noel spotted a comfortable reading chair, a mohair throw tossed over the back cushion, a floor lamp with three lights next to it, and a small filled bookcase.

"The one constant in my home is you'll find books everywhere. Feel free to look around and borrow whatever you wish to read."

"Thanks."

"Practical stuff," Justin said as he walked in behind Noel. "Through the door to the right of the tall dresser is a walk-in closet. The door on the left will take you to your bathroom."

"Shower," Noel said in an almost reverent tone.

Justin chuckled. "Take a long hot shower and change into some relaxing clothes. Put all your dirty clothes in the seabag and bring it downstairs. We'll see what we can save and run through the laundry."

"Don't know how much that will be."

"If we need to go to the store, we'll make the time to do so. Not saying how I wouldn't mind seeing you… Never mind," Justin said with a grin. "Meanwhile, I'll take a shower on my own."

Noel frowned at Justin's insistence on solo showers.

"I'll be downstairs to make dinner. We need to get you eating right for your diabetes. I picked up cookbooks from the store, so I know what you can eat. By the time I get food cooking, I'm sure the furry household members will put in an appearance."

"You don't have to change your lifestyle for me." Noel twisted to look at him.

"Nah, from what I noticed with the various recipes everything is something I can eat as long as I exchange regular dairy for soy products, so I don't mind the change. I can always do with less sugar in my life. Are you allergic to anything?"

Noel shook his head. "Nope."

"Good to know." Justin placed a hand on Noel's shoulder, squeezed in gentle comfort, then moved to the door and looked over his shoulder. "Please, make yourself at home. I want you to feel comfortable here, no more running."

Noel swallowed and stared at the floor. He lifted his gaze and met Justin's pine green gaze. "Thank you, Justin, for everything."

Stepping back to Noel, Justin leaned in and kissed him on the cheek. "You're more than welcome. Take a hot lingering shower. I have all kinds of delicious bath stuff you can indulge yourself with. Anything you need, feel free to use it. If not, we'll find something else." With a smile, he left and stopped. He pointed toward the left. "That side of the house is the master suite if you need me for anything. Okay?"

Noel nodded.

"Good. I'll see you in a few." Justin left and disappeared down the hallway.

Noel let out a long breath, his nerves a wreck after Justin had given him such a tender touch, and scrubbed a hand over his face. His shaking fingers touched his cheek where Justin's lips had met his skin.

Leaving the relaxing shower, Noel stretched his exhausted muscles, sore from a decent day of work and not stress from wondering where he would sleep for the night, or even if he would survive the night. He was safe, secure, clean, and soon to be fed. The abandoned safe-haven baby found a safe haven, a sanctuary against the cold and misery with Justin at the center. With a quick swipe of the towel against his hair to whisk away most of the moisture, he wrapped it around his hips while moving to the counter. He opened the black travel diabetes case and dealt with the testing procedures. He stashed his extra boxes of supplies in the bathroom's cabinet, but he would need to transfer the insulin bottles to the fridge.

The meter beeped and a low number appeared on a screen with a warning.

"Yeah, yeah, I know I'm in a low pattern. Sue me," Noel muttered as he dropped the used strip in the trash. Since he wasn't sure what Justin was preparing for dinner, he drew out a medium amount of insulin into the needle. He would adjust things before he hit bed.

He swiped the alcohol pad against the skin near his lower abdomen and pinched what flesh he could with three fingers. Without hesitation, he stuck himself and hit the plunger. Once the medicine was in him, he tossed the lancet and needle in a used laundry detergent bottle and cleaned up the rest of the medical waste. He didn't want to leave things lying around Justin's home, especially knowing there were curious cats.

Noel left the bathroom and stopped.

"Speaking of the cats..."

Two large gray striped balls of fluff curled in feline contentment on the pile of clothes he'd left on the comforter when he found clean pajamas amongst the items Justin purchased. One ball unwound and a head lifted enough to let out a long yawn complete with sharp white fangs and pink tongue. Bright amber eyes peered at him, staring him down.

"Yeah, this isn't good." Noel moved to the door. "Justin, a little help."

"What's up? Need another towel?" Justin called up the stairs, his voice faint.

"Found the fur balls."

"Good to know they made an appearance. Come on down, dinner is almost ready."

"Not good."

"What?"

Noel knocked his head against the doorframe. He stared back at the two gray piles with claws and teeth. "I need you to get up here."

"What?"

"Justin! Get up here!"

"Okay. Okay."

Noel banged the back of his head against the wood. He heard footsteps.

"I'm here. What's wrong? Did you find the cats? I said they're friendly." Justin wiped his hands on a kitchen towel. "What are you doing in a towel? Not that I mind... you're adorable."

Noel flushed under the compliment, but jabbed a thumb inside the room's direction. "It's been overrun with paws."

"Pardon? Paws?" Justin stepped into the doorway and looked. "Oh!" He laughed when one of the cats lifted their head. "This is why there's a rule in my house. Don't leave clothes lying around in piles. It's more fresh laundered ones warm from the dryer they prefer, but I guess they figured this pile would do due to the new scents. They needed to claim the new territory."

Noel propped his shoulder against the wall and crossed arms over his chest. "You should have warned me earlier. They made themselves cozy, have sharp teeth and claws, and don't know me. How about you take care of this problem?"

"Are you afraid of two little itty bitty pussycats?"

Noel eyed the furry terrors and back to Justin. "They're not little itty bitty anything."

Justin rapped the back of his fingers on Noel's bare abdomen and walked to the bed. "Marlowe, Raleigh, you goofballs. What are you doing in here, boys? Huh…" He made soft chuffs, meows, and other noises to the cats while he tucked the kitchen towel in a back pocket. He stretched out both hands and petted the soft heads, scratched behind the triangle ears until he elicited steady purrs. "There are my good boys. I see you introduced yourselves to Noel, mixed your scents all together, and gave him a fright. Huh?"

Noel continued to watch Justin interact with the cats. He lowered a hand until his fingers brushed lightly against his abdomen where Justin had hit him.

"Okay, boys, time to leave Noel alone. Off the bed. Marlowe, Raleigh, get down." Justin leaned over, lifted one cat, and scooped up the second. Both cats flopped boneless in his arms, the beautiful stripes of their gray, silver, and black patterned fur revealed.

Both cats meowed in protest as they dropped to the floor on their paws. They flicked fluffy tails. One with white tipped paws sat and licked a paw in defiance.

"Yeah, Raleigh, I know. I'll pay for my horrid behavior to you." Justin shook his head at the cat's actions.

"Thanks." Noel looked down at the felines and their gorgeous guardian.

"No problem. Marlowe is this one." Justin pointed to the one who began to wrap his sinuous length around Noel's ankles and purred for attention.

"Friendly sort." Noel bent down a little and scratched the cat behind the ears.

"Very much. You may end up finding him sleeping with you or curling next to you somewhere." Justin pointed to the other cat, cleaning a fluffy, white-toed paw. "This is Raleigh. He has four white paws, unlike his brother, who has strips everywhere except for his pure white tipped tail. Raleigh is more of an independent sort. He'll come to you when he's ready. You can pick up Marlowe and he'll flop over like a ragdoll, hence their breed's name."

Noel continued to stroke the affectionate Marlowe.

"As much as I enjoy seeing the vast array of skin," Justin said as he moved closer and Noel rose from the crouch, holding onto the towel. He leaned close enough to take a deliberate sniff. "Hmm. Smell damn good too."

"Is it better than the forest and dirt odor?"

"Much much more divine." Justin pressed his lips against the back of Noel's nape.

Noel shivered under the gentle, foretelling touch.

"Get dressed before I forget myself."

"What if I want you to?"

"Not yet. We must take care of your health first. Besides, we need to learn about one another. I'm not a one-night stand kinda man." Justin pressed another kiss against Noel's skin. "Damn, you're so soft."

"Justin..."

Clearing his throat hard, Justin straightened and stepped back. "I'll let you get dressed. Bring your clothes down and we'll start the laundry. Come on, boys, I have dinner waiting for you." He moved to the door.

Noel met Justin's steady, admiring gaze over his lean frame, a little gaunt from his time on the streets.

"We need to put some weight and muscle on you. Get you back on the mend. Remove the shadows from your eyes," Justin said as he pressed his fingers to Noel's abdomen, chest, and then his cheeks. "You'll be even more of a looker."

Noel flushed dark under the praise.

Justin drew his finger along the edge of Noel's cheekbone and jaw. "Come downstairs when you're ready."

After swallowing with the gentle touch scorching sensitive nerves, Noel managed to nod. "Oh. Okay."

"Come on, boys, I know you want some dinner," Justin called to the cats.

Two fluffy tails followed him.

With a heavy sigh, Noel dropped to the edge of the bed, pressed a hand to his chest where his heart pounded from attraction and arousal. "Oh man, I'm in trouble."

Chapter Five

When the alarm went off next to him, Noel moaned and mumbled, not wanting to leave the warm nest and best sleep ever. He rubbed his cheek against the pillow and sighed. Everything that happened to him filled his brain—BookWorm, Justin, a job, a warm bed to sleep in, a pair of cats for companionship, and a chance for a better life.

With a smile, he woke and tried to move. His ass was hot as hell and something pushed him deeper into the mattress. Not to mention, a deep vibration moved through him and it wasn't one of those pleasant kinds tucked up against a gland. This was different.

He tried to twist his upper body, but could only turn his head to look over his head. Noel groaned. A purring sleeping Marlowe curled across his body. The cat yawned, stretched and pushed fluffy claws against Noel's butt-cheeks and flicked his tail.

Noel caught a glimpse of something red beyond Marlowe's fluffy body.

"Could you move, please?" Noel asked the feline.

The cat yawned again and purred.

"Yes, I see the fangs and know you're comfortable. I need you to move, please."

Marlowe lowered his head as if to fall back asleep.

"Nope. Sorry, I can't be your human pillow." Noel tilted his hips enough to disrupt the cat's balance.

With a mewl of complaint, Marlowe moved to the bed. He sat up almost regal, tail wrapped around him.

When Marlowe moved, Noel stared at the oversized box tied with a bright red ribbon placed on the end of the bed. A red envelope was on top. Flipping back the covers, he crawled down the bed to study the box.

He tilted his head to the box and asked the cat, "Do you know anything about this?"

The cat gave him a steady look.

Noel shifted to a sitting position next to the box. He lifted the red envelope and slid a finger under the golden seal. Inside was a single-sided red and ivory linen card. He read the gorgeous black calligraphy writing.

On the 7th Day of Christmas, my Safe Haven Gave to Me:
Warmth of the Season!
~Your Secret Santa

"What is this all about?"

Marlowe didn't answer him other than to flick his tail.

"What is your guardian up to this morning? He's being rather sneaky. Seventh day of Christmas. He knows I'm not a fan of the holidays. Why would he put that on a card?" Noel untied the ribbon. He lifted the lid and the tissue paper. "Oh—"

Inside the box lay a wooly knit scarf, leather gloves, and a leather jacket. Everything was brand spanking new. Noel extracted the jacket and slid off the bed to pull it on over the soft cotton pajamas Justin had picked up for him. The coat's hem hit him mid-thigh, lined for snugness and protection, weathered against the elements, and fit him to perfection. He loved the deep chocolate brown color. He lifted both sleeves to his nose and breathed in the scent of rich, pungent leather.

"Oh, Justin." He sat down hard, picked up the card, and stared at the note again.

Removing the coat and laying it out on the bed, he raced into the bathroom. This morning he didn't have to rush through cleaning up and getting ready. He could be relaxed and leisure. No one would shout and kick him out. He took care of his morning testing, brushed his teeth with the new brush and paste, and styled his hair.

Holy crap, I can actually style my hair!

He felt almost giddy. With a couple of messy soft spikes to one side, he ran his fingers through the rest. There was even a fresh stick of deodorant and a couple options of body sprays and colognes. He slicked up his underarms and tested some of the bottles. He went with a spicy scent this morning to see if he liked it.

All styled, he headed to the bedroom and the mostly empty walk-in closet. Justin had helped him move the dresser inside the walk-in closet and showed him how to organize everything between the walk-in shelves, racks, and dresser drawers. As he listened and followed suggestions, Noel hung, folded, and laid out the different clothes, shoes, and accessories Justin had purchased for him. Once laundered, his older, rattier clothes were on the other side.

This morning, he selected a pair of brown chinos, a cream long-sleeve Henley shirt, and a soft patterned sweater with the same brown and a rich green. He added a dark brown belt and leather boots.

OMG, I love selecting clothes to wear. I can't wait till I can find more clothes.

He pulled on clean boxers, another favorite thing, and changed into the new outfit. He smoothed everything down with his hands to make sure there were no wrinkles or balls of fuzz. He folded the pajamas and placed them on the shelf. He grabbed his messenger bag, which looked so forlorn against the rest of the new items, and returned to the bed.

Marlowe remained on the bed, grooming himself in a lazy kitten fashion.

Noel scratched the cat behind one triangle ear to elicit another purr. He then upended the bag and spilled out all of the contents. He grabbed the traveling kit first and went to the bathroom to refresh the diabetes supplies. With that part taken care of, he sorted out and cleaned things he didn't need or wouldn't have to use in this new life. As with everything in his life, he would need to restock most of the basic stuff.

When he closed the bag, he smoothed his hand over the cover. He had been through so much with this bag over his shoulder. Ever since he pulled it out of a bin at a thrift store and fixed it. Even if he got a new bag, he would keep this somewhere as a reminder of where he'd been and where he was headed in life. He would never forget where he started.

With that set in his head, he slid the messenger bag over one shoulder, gathered his new presents, and headed downstairs. A soft thump of paws told him Marlowe trailed him.

When he reached the kitchen and saw Justin making breakfast at the stove, looking damn stylish in his own right, Noel left his gifts and bag on a chair. He couldn't make a big deal of the gift, somehow feeling Justin would hate it. He wandered over to the coffee machine and poured himself a plain black cup of coffee. Since he could, he stirred in some sugar. A step to one side, he lifted on his toes, and kissed the man's cheek and went to sit down for breakfast. It seemed to be the right choice when Justin ducked his head with a blush.

Noel smiled into the cup and enjoyed the simple morning routine with Justin.

Since there wasn't a delivery for Noel to concentrate on for most of the morning, he covered the floor and assisted all the customers while Justin handled the register. They both decided it was too crazy of a time to teach him how the darn thing worked and Noel didn't trust himself with the responsibility.

Throughout the morning, they made a good team. It wasn't hectic crazy, but the rush was steady to keep them occupied and on their toes.

The four-block based shopping plaza was designed for customers to drift and move from one place to the next. All parking lots were beyond the plaza, including the deliveries and staff, not to disrupt the flow or ambiance. The customers walked on a patterned brick layout with different shades of bricks. Copper poles filled the area with enough light in the evenings along with the lanterns placed along the pathways. Different landscaping arrangements added color to match the benches and fountains. Music drifted from hidden speakers.

As the morning slid to afternoon, a light amount of snow drifted down from the gray skies, but didn't disrupt the holiday atmosphere.

With a break in the customers, Noel stared out the front bay window at the activity beyond the shop. He intended to change out the display of books on this side for a different arrangement, but got distracted.

"Look at that. A bit of snow," Justin said as he stopped behind Noel.

A little startled, Noel almost fell off the bench. Instead, the books in his arms toppled every which way on him.

"Sorry. Guess you were lost in your thoughts," Justin said with a soft chuckle. He bent to help re-stack the books.

"Where did you disappear too?"

"We received a box of goodies from one of the bakeries. I set it up in the back. Go and help yourself if you're hungry."

"I'll check them out in a bit."

Justin looked at the book and the half-empty window shelves. "Are you changing the display?"

"If you don't mind, I thought I could move stuff around," Noel said. "These have been here for a week. To offset the different books as a gift side, I wanted to fill this up with fantasy and paranormal books."

"What an excellent idea. These could draw folks in, give them an escape to the craziness of shopping and the season. I like it," Justin said.

"Oh, perfect. I should have asked first—"

Justin waved away his concern. "I have some decorative pieces that would help go with it."

"Sure, anything to help fill things up. Then I got distracted by people-watching and the snow." He settled back on the bench to look outside.

"Are you also thinking about still being stuck out there?"

Noel nodded as he nibbled on his lower lip.

"It could be a while before things sink in that your life is changing," Justin said as he placed his hand on Noel's shoulder.

"Thanks for taking a chance on me," Noel said as he met Justin's gaze.

"Thanks for accepting my help," Justin said and tapped his knuckles lightly on Noel's chin. "I'll bring these books back to the shelves and return with some of my favorites. We'll work on this together between customers."

"Gonna show me all your skills?"

Justin laughed as he disappeared amongst the tall wooden stacks.

Noel smiled and the bell chimed as more customers entered the shop. He set his handful of books down and went to offer his assistance.

When their shift ended and Justin drove them home, Noel dropped his messenger bag on the floor and flopped across the sofa with a huff of exhaustion. His new boots hung off the edge.

"Don't wanna move ever again. All hurts..." Noel said with a whimper.

Justin looked down at him and chuckled in amusement. "Sorry. Five more shopping days."

Noel moaned, grabbed a pillow, and shoved it against his face. He scrambled to keep it in place when Justin tugged it away. He gave him a playful growl.

"Come on, get up and moving. Take a shower if you want. Go change into something comfortable and help me get dinner. I'll show you a way to relax after we eat and zone out on some television," Justin said.

"Slave driver," Noel called out.

"You wouldn't have it any other way."

That would be an oh-hell-yeah since Noel didn't want to go back near the old way of living day-to-day on the edge of despair and loss. He rolled off the couch, grabbed his bag, and followed Justin upstairs.

After dinner, Justin tugged him back onto the sofa, only this time Noel curled against his side. Content as all hell, he happily snuggled closer as Justin flipped through different stations. Since he hadn't watched television in years and didn't know much about any of the shows, Noel let himself drift off as Justin selected one.

A soft kiss upon his lips woke him up.

Noel blinked and looked into Justin's green gaze. "Do that again," he murmured.

"Are you sure?"

Noel lifted his fingers to trace Justin's lower face. "Yes."

As he moved closer, Noel lifted up until their lips pressed again into the gentlest kiss of exploring one another. A soft moan came from one of them. Noel realized he made it as Justin swept his tongue along Noel's lower lip.

The kiss deepened, gradual and slow, but nothing further.

How he wanted more from this man.

Instead, Justin pulled away, his eyes dark with passion. "Time we go to bed."

"You promised me a way to relax."

"If you get any more relaxed, you'll be limper than spaghetti."

Noel chuckled. "Sorry. I know. I left the pasta too long. Next time I'll get it right."

"It's okay. Takes a while to learn what al dente means," Justin teased and feathered another kiss on Noel's lips. "Bed. This time I mean it." He pushed away and held his hand out to pull Noel to his feet.

"Together?"

"Nope."

Noel sighed but followed Justin through the darkened hall until they reached his door first. He stopped when Justin tucked him against the frame for another soft kiss. He moaned, lifted on his toes to meet him fully.

"Hmm. So sweet. Sleep. Good night," Justin whispered and left him alone.

His body ached, hard and needy, from the tempting kisses. Noel thumped his head against the nearest wall, but did as ordered. He crawled into bed, under the thick warm covers, and fell fast asleep. He dreamed of sweet kisses and pine-green eyes.

Chapter Six

The next morning, six more days to Christmas, Noel woke to another red envelope lying on the bed. There was no box with it, just the large red envelope. Unlike yesterday, Marlowe tucked himself against Noel's side to sleep and purred as Noel awakened. Somehow, the cat seemed to have adopted him. Not minding that in the least, he gave Marlowe some attention; he found himself used to the cat's comforting presence.

"What do we have this morning?"

With a head butt against his fingers, Marlow lowered his head back on his paws.

Noel slid his finger under the golden seal and pulled out the new card.

On the 6th Day of Christmas, my Safe Haven Gave to Me:
Comforts of the Season!
~Your Secret Santa

Also inside the envelope, he discovered a voucher for a full day at the local salon. He grimaced at the thought of being scrubbed and plucked within an inch of his life. Behind the voucher, he found several gift cards to various clothing stores.

Curious as to how far Justin would go with his plans, Noel fell out of the bed and raced to the closet. He yanked it open and dropped his jaw.

"No, he didn't. When did he sneak in here to do this?"

Even the old tattered clothes he saved and laundered were now missing from the shelves and drawers. Only the few new clothes remained in the closet, looking lonely and pitiful.

"What am I going to wear? I don't have enough..."

Noel stared at the envelope filled with gift cards.

"Too much, Justin. Please..." Noel closed his eyes and held the envelope to his chest. "Don't break my heart. Please." He pressed a kiss to the envelope and tucked it into his messenger bag.

He went through his morning routines in the bathroom, cleaning, testing, primping, and styling to make himself better every day. Shiny and smelling good, he went to the closet and perused the minimal choices.

This time he paired slim fitting tan chinos with a French cuff dress shirt in blue and finished with a deep hunter green cardigan. He accessorized the outfit with the same dark leather belt and boots.

Once dressed, he grabbed the bag and went downstairs. Marlowe had already left, repulsed when Noel dashed off the bed and jolted him.

As he did yesterday, he dropped off his messenger bag, filled his cup of coffee, and kissed Justin's cheek. Though this time, he whispered in a teasing tone, "You're a sneaky thief."

Justin glanced over to him and smiled. "Nothing could save those hopeless pieces of cloth and you know it. No other choice."

"Did you have to toss everything?"

"Every last thread and button."

"What am I going to wear when I'm not in these clothes? I only have the one pair of pajamas."

"What was in the envelope?"

"Don't you know?"

Justin gave him a secretive smile.

"Gift cards to different stores."

"Excellent. Then we'll go shopping this afternoon."

"We're exhausted after the shift."

"I spoke with Jamie and William. We're taking off an hour earlier to shop."

"Justin…"

Justin lifted a finger and pressed it to Noel's lips. "You promised you wouldn't fight me or protest. I'm calling on you now to remember that promise."

Noel blinked, pulled back any more protests, and went to sit at the table. He kept quiet throughout breakfast and the drive to the bookstore.

As he'd come to expect, the bookstore was crazy with the mad rush of shoppers going in and out, searching for the perfect gift. He couldn't figure out some people and why they tried so damn hard for a few minutes of surprise.

Exhausted and never happier to see Jamie entering the store and take over for them, Noel draped his body in one of the office chairs. He drank a bottle of water from Justin's secret stash.

"That was a mad rush. I can't believe how well the store is doing. It appears more folks are shopping the smaller businesses instead of large chains," Justin said as he entered the office, grabbed a bottle, and dropped in the chair next to Noel.

"I could sleep for a week."

With a laugh, Justin toasted him with the opened bottle. "I can do the same. We'll sleep after the holidays."

"Promise?"

"We won't have much of a choice."

Groaning, Noel leaned back against the chair. "Can we go home?" Hearing a strange noise, he turned and saw Justin staring at him. "What?"

"You called my place home."

Noel straightened and thought about what he said. "Oh. I did."

"Thank you for thinking of my place as home."

Noel shrugged and blushed. "I feel... safe."

"Good to know I'm on the right path."

"Why are you giving me these envelopes?"

"You'll find out at the end."

"Can't you tell me?"

Justin shook his head. "Would you like to see what the voucher and those cards can give you?" He rolled to a sitting position and checked his watch. "Yup, it's four o'clock and we can head outta here early to hit the stores."

"A shopping trip? Now?"

"Yup, it's the best kind of trip. As you figured out this morning, we're replacing your wardrobe. No more dressing like a bum."

"I was a bum..."

"You were a survivor. That's different."

"Nothing too crazy," Noel said.

"I promise."

"No spa yet. Please."

"No. No. You need more than a quick trip. We'll go after the holiday."

"Good. I'm not sure if I like the idea of being scrubbed, plucked, and wrapped with god knows what."

Laughing, Justin tugged Noel out of the chair, hugged him off his feet. "If it makes you feel better, I'll order the same package so we can do it together."

"It might help a little bit."

"Come on, get your stuff and let's get out of here. We need to go shopping," Justin said.

With a laugh at Justin's enthusiasm, Noel followed as Justin took him on a whirlwind shopping tour to use the various cards.

Chapter Seven

The shopping trip took longer than either of them expected. Of course, it was all Justin's fault because he kept adding to the piles and totals. When Justin was on a roll, Noel learned there was no stopping him.

They ended up eating during the whirlwind so Noel could test and administer his insulin. Once finished, they hauled the loot into the house and Justin helped him clip the tags, launder what they needed too, and organize everything in the closet and drawers. There remained room to expand his wardrobe. Things were getting better.

Both of them crawled into their beds and fell asleep, and Noel awakened the next morning and slapped his hand on the alarm clock. He buried his face under the pillows and ignored the warm weight dropping on his ass.

Marlowe made his intentions known. He purred and kneaded Noel's butt with his fluffy paws. Noel waved a hand behind him to discourage the feline. Marlowe continued his kneading.

With a shove of the pillow, Noel glared at the cat over his shoulder. "Do you mind? Didn't we talk about this the first morning? My butt isn't a cat pillow."

Marlowe meowed.

"What? Your food is downstairs. I don't have it."

The answer was another meow.

"Really? I don't understand cat."

Sharp pricks dug into his ass.

"Ouch! You furry brat!" Noel shouted as he twisted hard to dislodge the annoying feline. He rubbed his tortured ass with one hand.

The door burst inside with Justin rushing into the room. Marlowe fluffed, leapt down, and raced away.

Justin watched the fleeing feline and Noel. "What the hell..."

Noel glared at Justin. "Your cat dug his claws in my butt."

"What?"

"Your. Feline. Dug. Claws. In. My. ASS!" Noel repeated in slow modulated words to make them crisp and clean.

"Umm. Oh. Ouch?"

Noel narrowed his gaze.

"What happened to make him dig his claws into such a tender spot?"

"How should I know? He's a cat!"

Justin dragged a hand through his hair. He pulled a red envelope from his back pocket and tossed it on the bed.

Noel stared at the envelope and back to Justin.

"I'm sorry about Marlowe's behavior. I'm sure he wanted you to get up with him."

"We talked earlier about him sleeping on my butt. I didn't appreciate being a pillow, but curling next to me was good."

"He slept on your butt."

"And purred. Not the type of vibration I want back there, hmm?" Noel said with a pointed tone.

"I'll remember that for later." With a grin, Justin pointed to the envelope. "I forgot to drop this off earlier while you were asleep. Sorry to ruin the whole 'Secret Santa' thing."

"Umm. Yeah. About that." Noel tilted his lips to one side in an answering grin. "There are only two of us in this house along with two felines. I don't think the cats know how to write or purchase these things. I'm not dumb."

"No. No. Didn't think that, just..."

"You wanted to keep the magic and suspense."

Justin nodded. "Perhaps to make up for the time when you were a kid and didn't experience all of this around the holiday."

"You are and this is better than if I was a kid. I've never had anything like this happen to me." Noel curled forward and picked up envelope. He broke the golden seal and pulled out the card.

On the 5th Day of Christmas, my Safe Haven Gave to Me:
Sounds of the Season!
~Your Secret Santa

Reading it again, Noel lifted it with a wave. "What's this?"

"You'll find out after work. Make sure you dress warm. We'll be outside for a while tonight."

Noel flapped the card against his forehead. "What are you doing to me?"

"Showing you the other side of this holiday," Justin said. "Come downstairs for breakfast. We need to get going." He left the room, calling for Marlowe in a sharp tone.

After he dropped back on the bed, Noel pressed the pillow to his face and screamed. With the release, he rolled out of bed, showered, took care of his testing, and primped and styled himself.

He wandered back to the closet and stared at his options. "Warm. Dress warm."

This time from the array of clothes, he hopped on one foot and the other to tug on gray socks. He stepped into charcoal gray trousers and slid a black leather belt through the loops, but didn't fasten it. He chose a rich purple silk shirt and tugged it over his head. He tucked it in place and fastened the belt. He finished the outfit with an Irishman knit sweater in a pebbled beige color. Since Justin said they were standing outside, he grabbed the new brown felt fedora from the shelf, picked up black boots, and left the closet. He managed to sling one hand under the messenger bag and scrambled downstairs. Even during the shopping trip, he remained reluctant to replace the bag.

With a yawn at the unexpected wake-up, he craved lots of hot coffee this morning. He also owed Marlowe an apology. He entered the kitchen, set all his things down, and went for his first cup of coffee. He stirred and leaned to give Justin a kiss on the cheek.

"What was that for?" Justin asked as he stopped in mid-movement.

"Been doing it every morning, don't want to screw up the momentum," Noel said with a grin.

"Hmm. I like this arrangement." Justin checked out his outfit as he did every morning. "Excellent job once again. Shoes?"

"The sleek black ankle boots you insisted I get."

"Ahh, good choice and you needed them. You already had the brown ones and you like them, why not the black ones?"

"Since you taught me to dress classy with fun, I added a bit of unexpected color," Noel said and pulled the sweater's sleeve up to reveal the purple.

"Perfect touch."

With a chuckle, Noel went to the table. He clucked and coaxed Marlowe to come over. He whispered and loved on the cat until it melted against his legs, purring with enthusiasm. "No more butt sleeping or claws, okay, buddy? We'll get along fine. I promise."

Justin laughed as Noel sweet-talked Marlowe, until Raleigh butted his way in for some scratching and attention. The rest of the morning started splendid afterward.

With the crazy day finishing, Justin looked up when Noel chuckled. He saw William cross another day on the large December calendar in his office with a huge red "X." The older gentleman left the office with a wave.

"Enjoy your date," he called out.

With a grin, Justin ducked his head and concentrated on his paperwork again.

"Date?" Noel asked.

Thanks a lot, William.

"What else should we call it?" Justin paused and lifted his gaze again. "We're together. We're going out. I'm interested in dating you, getting to know you. Don't you feel the same?"

"Umm. Yes."

"Then it's a date. Give me a second to finish tallying these receipts," Justin said.

As he tallied and dropped the numbers for most of the day, he glanced up at times and saw Noel moving about as he finished up the day. Within moments, Noel gathered his messenger bag, coat, and hat and sat in the chair.

That messenger bag, the last link to his past. Justin studied the battered and torn bag that didn't work with all the new things in Noel's life. Still, Noel kept a tight hold on that precious bag. He refused multiple times to consider getting a new one during their shopping spree.

Justin decided to let the argument go and not push Noel further. Noel would make the decision on his own when he was comfortable with the changes.

"Okay. Done. Jamie needs to add the rest when he closes and drop everything at the bank," he said as he zipped the bank envelope and tossed it in the safe. He closed it and spun the lock.

When he got up and stretched, Justin felt a heated gaze upon him. He glanced to find Noel staring at him. He looked to see his sweater and undershirt rose above his waist to reveal some skin.

Noel blushed when he thought Justin caught him.

"There's no reason to be embarrassed at being attracted to someone. You're not stuck in the shadows anymore. You can have whatever feelings you want."

"What happens when they're for someone unattainable?"

"Why would you consider anyone unattainable for you? You're a strong, wonderful young man who overcame a lot of difficulties in life. You're a catch in my eyes," Justin said as he tucked his undershirt back in place. He wound the scarf around his neck, slid his arms into the sleeves of his coat, and buttoned it up.

Without a word, Noel tugged the scarf and gloves from the messenger bag. He folded the scarf in half, wrapped it around his neck, and threaded the tails through the loop to make a simple knot of soft warm cotton and wool against his neck. He buttoned the coat, but tucked the gloves in a pocket. With the fedora in place, he followed Justin out of the office, weaving through customers and stacks.

Justin waved to Jamie and William and opened the door for Noel. They stepped outside into the chilly night. He clasped their hands together and led him away from their usual parking lot. He hoped Noel would enjoy their evening out. They moved through the crowds toward the far side of the plaza.

"Where are we going?"

"You'll see," Justin said and spotted a familiar vendor on the corner. "Want some hot chocolate?"

"Please."

With a nod, he stopped them at a street vendor. "Hi, Leroy, how's business this evening?"

"Good to see you, Mr. Justin. It's getting better as the night gets colder, sir. What can I getcha?" the grizzled African-American man asked with a smile.

"One of your finest hot chocolates with whip cream for my friend. One soy peppermint chocolate for me," he ordered.

"One of the few who order these soy things," Leroy said with a chuckle and gave him a total.

"You know me. At least you cater to us non-lactose folks." Justin handed over cash and tucked a couple of dollars in the tip cup. "Sorry, this skipped over me. Leroy, this is Noel. You might have seen him wandering around last few weeks."

"Yes, I have seen this youngster. You're looking a might better," Leroy said with a nod as he fixed the hot drinks.

"Thanks. I'm feeling better." Noel nodded toward Justin. "It's all his doing."

Justin grinned and shrugged. "Just gave him a job."

"Good for you, young fella. Couldn't find a better fella to work for around here." Leroy added a playful high swirl of cream on Noel's cup and handed it over. "Here you go."

"Thank you," Noel said and held the cup in both hands.

Justin waited for the reaction as Noel took a sip. Noel closed his eyes and moaned.

"Oh wow, what is in this?" Noel asked as he opened his eyes. "It's so velvety smooth and rich."

"I don't use that powder stuff, youngster. You want chocolate, you gets it," Leroy said and finished Justin's cup with a peppermint stick and handed it over. "Enjoy the festivities."

"See you later," Justin said and led Noel away from the friendly vendor. "He's been selling hot drinks for longer than I can remember. He offers everything from different flavors of chocolate, to cider, mulled wine, eggnog, and different teas. His chai tea is full of spice and delicious."

"What other chocolate drinks?"

"He has a crazy Mexican spiced cocoa drink that's spicy with smoked chipotles, this peppermint has a stick and oil, malted cocoa with toasted marshmallows, minty hot cocoa with mint leaves and a scoop of mint chocolate chip ice cream and just about anything else. It's a tradition to stop by his cart to see what he offers."

Noel sipped more from his cup and nodded. "We'll have to stop more often. This is delicious."

Justin chuckled. "I think we can accomplish that. That's his basic double cocoa for you. I wanted to start you with the original."

"Good choice," Noel said as he licked the cream.

Justin laughed and playfully cleaned Noel's nose with a swipe of his finger to remove the cream. He held his finger between them and looked at the cream. As much as he wanted to, he couldn't indulge himself. Noel licked away the cream with a smile. Justin growled at the move. He wanted the moment to last longer.

Instead, they continued to walk.

Noel pointed to the different areas and asked, "What's happening around here?"

Justin explained the different traditions offered for the shoppers and locals' enjoyment. There was an ice-carving contest where folks worked huge hunks of clear ice into fabulous sculptures with chainsaws, hammers, and precise carving tools as everyone watched.

The kid corner set in Santa's Workshop gave kids a chance to create different things on any given night, from ornaments, to decorations and gifts while their parents shopped. All the children were well watched by the elves and matched to a parent with special wristbands before they could leave. It was a good system since no one ever went missing.

At the end, they stopped at a small stage where a crowd started to gather and fill the benches.

"Here we are. This is our stop," Justin said as he guided and scooted Noel down one of the rows and plopped on a bench. They huddled together, hot cups nestled in their hands as they listened to the Carols Wars.

"What are we doing here?"

With a smile at the question, Justin looked over to him. "Every holiday season, the call would go out for folks to create caroling groups and join the wars. Each night, different pairs will take the stage and sing a medley carols to one another. The audience with a trio of judges decides who goes to the next round. This happens up to the finals night on the twenty-third."

"Then what happens?"

"On Christmas Eve, the winning group takes the stage on their own for the entire night to carol the crowd. Also, a special Snow Narrator gets on stage with them and reads the Christmas story, mostly to the kids, but everyone listens. The carolers help add tunes and extras to the story."

Noel fell silent for a moment and looked around them. He returned his gaze to Justin. "This town really gets into the spirit."

"Yeah, it's great."

"This is what you meant on the card."

Justin nodded.

"How long does all this happen?"

"It starts with the first weekend of December when they light the huge tree in the center and all the lights in the plaza. All the stores have to be ready with their decorations and turned on the same time."

Noel looked over at him. "You love this place."

Justin lowered his gaze and nodded. "It's my home. The one I chose." He tucked his arm around Noel to bring them closer. "I hope you enjoy tonight and see the other side of the holidays. One that is warm and giving. There's something else to all the craziness going on at the store with the shopping."

As the music started, they fell silent and listened.

Chapter Eight

When he woke the following morning with Marlowe curled against his side once more, Noel wondered what his Secret Santa had conjured this time inside the red envelope. Every day at BookWorm got busier as Christmas got closer and customers became more frantic with finding the right gifts. More and more, Noel ran around the store with a customer. Together, they hunted for either a precise book or series. With book in hand, the customer joined the line at the register.

Noel couldn't believe how much he loved working there. He dreaded his other jobs and knew why. Those old ones were a means to an end, to keep him in the tiny room and enough food to eat.

This time around, things were flexible. He didn't have to work to survive. Justin, William, and Jamie were the best coworkers and taught him there could be more than making an earning for a simple room and food. Working at the store meant he could connect to different customers, lovers of reading and stories, and be himself.

Coming home with Justin was the highlight of every day.

As he curled into a sitting position, giving Marlowe a scratch behind his ears, Noel found his red envelope. He picked it up and slid open the golden seal. Pulling out the card, he read the note.

On the 4th Day of Christmas, my Safe Haven Gave to Me:
The Wonderful Scents of the Season!
~Your Secret Santa

"Okay? What is this one?" Noel showed the cat the cryptic note, which didn't have an accompanying gift card or anything.

The cat meowed.

"Fine, I'll go and ask."

Noel went through his regular morning routines and headed to the walk-in closet.

"One of the other best times of the day, Mr. Marlowe-cat. I get to find something I want to wear, not what I have to wear. Fresh, bright fabrics full of color. No stains, no dirt, no nastiness whatsoever. Underwear. Hell, I get clean underwear every freaking day," Noel said as he slid on new briefs. He wasn't sure whether he was a boxers or briefs man. There were too many different kinds and he wanted to try them all.

He hopped as he tugged on plain socks. Then he stepped into cream-colored Dockers, tugged a cream Henley shirt over his head and tucked it in. He slid a blue canvas belt through the loops and secured it. He slipped his arms into a French blue shirt, buttoned all the way down, and tucked it in, muttering about forgetting the belt. He finished off with a tailored waistcoat vest and the brown leather boots he'd been favoring.

With a bounce to his step, he grabbed the card, along with the rest of his things, and headed downstairs. This time he followed the high furry tail as Marlowe went to find his breakfast.

He dropped his things and went to get his first cup of coffee, settling into their morning routines. He tapped the card on the counter next to Justin. "What's this?"

Justin looked over from the omelet pan and shook his head. "You'll see after work."

"Justin!"

"After work," Justin insisted and plated both omelets and bacon. "Now eat so we can get going. As we get closer, the days are going to get worse. They always do." He sat in the chair next to Noel and dug into his omelet and coffee.

With a groan, Noel did the same.

As Justin predicted, the store was jam packed from the moment they opened the doors. Noel raced through the stacks with customers, helped them find books and gifts, not bothering with stocking shipments unless they ran out of certain titles and went to the back to retrieve those requested titles. Justin remained tied to the register until William came in, an hour earlier than usual, bringing lunch for them on his dime. Both of them wolfed down their food in the back, Justin forced Noel to pause and check his levels while they took a needed break off their feet, and laughed at the craziness out on the floor. Jamie arrived early too, saying William had called him in to help.

"As usual, people are getting crazier as the days wind down to Christmas. You would think people would get a little wiser about shopping, but nope. Never happens, just the usual craziness every year." Justin rubbed a hand over the back of his neck.

"Why do people do this to themselves? It's stupid." Noel finished his injection and tossed his needle in the container. He no longer cared if Justin watched him during lunchtime. There was no way he was leaving the backroom to push through the crowds to get to the bathroom. After he packed his kit together, he put it back in the messenger bag inside the locker. Then he returned to his seat near Justin.

"I have no clue, I learned to go with the flow and drink copious amounts of caffeine to get through the day. Is everything good with your blood sugar levels?"

"For now, yeah, I'm dealing with them."

"That doesn't sound promising to me. What's going on?"

"My levels are jumpy and not steadying like they should from one test to the next. I'm keeping track of them in my journal like I'm supposed to," Noel said as he traced useless patterns across the table.

Justin captured Noel's fingers in his and held them still. "What will help you? Other than not working crazy hours like we have this week."

"I guess getting in to see a doctor like you mentioned. Eat a few snacks in between meals to regulate my intake and sugars."

"What about those diabetic snacks and shakes I see in the stores or commercials? Would those work for you?"

"Wouldn't hurt to try them and see."

"Okay. We'll pick some up and you can start. I don't mind if you munch on the floor, just not in front of a customer."

"Yeah, it wouldn't look nice to turn around with a mouth full of food when a customer asks for help."

Justin snorted in amusement and squeezed Noel's hand. "As for a doctor, I'm working with my store's health carrier to get you added to the coverage, but they're giving me crap about being outside the regular sign-ups or some shit."

Noel glanced at him. "What?"

"William, Jamie, and I are on it, so it'll be easy to add you on the plan."

"I have an existing condition and they'll shoot your premiums sky-high."

"I'll worry about it, not you."

"Just—"

Justin waved away his concerns and rose to his feet. "Let's go face the crazed masses."

"Ugh." Noel banged his forehead on the table. "Oww..."

Justin chuckled and held out his hand. "I'll stay in the stacks with you and leave Jamie and William up front."

"Okay." Noel laced his fingers with Justin.

Together, they trudged out to face the holiday shoppers once more for another five hours of madness.

Two hours later than their scheduled time, Justin managed to get both of them out of the store. They were dead on their feet as they climbed into the Soul. "Sorry about going over the clock."

"I don't mind. Not like I have anywhere else to go," Noel said. "You're my ride."

"True, but that doesn't mean I like to take advantage of my employees." Justin tapped his fingers a few times on the wheel.

Noel pulled the red card from his messenger bag. He flapped it against Justin's arm. "Are you going to tell me anything about this now? You look like you have something to say."

Justin glanced at the card and back to Noel. "The card has something to do with a little tradition I honor around this time. This year, I wanted to include you on everything. I usually start my personal traditions around this time."

"What is this tradition?"

"I visit the local Christmas tree lot, pick out my favorite, bring it home, and put it up."

"Four days before Christmas? Are any left?"

"Around here, yup, and they get the last fresh supply from their farm. It's all local based. The tree farm is up in the local mountains."

"Must be convenient."

"For the tree lot owners, yup, and I'm guaranteed a fresh Christmas tree that hasn't been lying around."

"Once you get the tree, what happens? Do you decorate it on your own?"

"Nope, I have better plans." Justin gave him a quick grin.

"Of course you do. What is it?"

"Everyone from the store, a few of the store's regulars, our Addicts, and other friends comes over the day before Christmas Eve. This year it will be Sunday evening, after we close the store at two. Anyway, we all decorate, exchange little nonsense gifts, and enjoy a party."

"Oh, yeah, I heard you mention the party to a few customers." Noel looked out the window and tapped the card against the window.

Up until now, all the cards Justin created had been to help Noel and bring gifts into his life. He wondered how Noel would take this one since the card was for the both of them and expanded beyond them.

"Sunday's my birthday," Noel said in a muttered tone.

"I remember you telling me that."

"This isn't a birthday party, right?"

Justin shook his head. "No. I wouldn't push you into that. There was something else I've been considering for you."

"You've been doing a lot of that," Noel said, a bit of sarcasm in his tone.

"Smart ass." Justin smacked his fingers against Noel's knee. "We need to get you set with a new bank account and everything. Do you want to take care of this first? We could use my bank. They're still open, and you would feel better with a little cash in your wallet. We can get you a debit card."

"You don't mind?"

Justin shook his head as he drove. "Not at all. Did I upset you by mentioning the tree and party? If you don't want to do any of this, I will back off. I promise."

"No, let's go to the bank and the tree lot." Noel flipped the card between his fingers. "Perhaps it's time to change my thoughts about the holiday. I've been holding on to all the bad stuff that happened around this time. Could it be holding me back?"

"It could act as a deterrent, force you to put up walls. Let's start breaking those walls then. Are you ready to pick out the first scent of the season?" Justin moved a hand from the wheel to Noel's knee.

"You know I've never purchased gifts," Noel admitted, "picked out a tree, or gone to a Christmas party."

"I'll help you with everything. We can start small. Perhaps you could get a gift for William and Jamie. They were asking about something for you."

"Really? They asked to get me something?"

"Yes, they both love working with you. You do a wonderful job at the store and they see it." Justin grinned while he drove away from the plaza to reach his bank and the food store.

"Okay, yeah, I want to find something for them. What about you? I need to find something special for you."

"I don't expect—"

Noel interrupted. "Nope, I gotta find something."

Justin chuckled. "I'll leave it up to you."

"The cats need a gift."

"You want to get them a gift?"

"I enjoy waking up to my purring alarm. It's funny to see where Marlowe curled against me during the night."

"We're out of their favorite catnip. They love dried tuna treats. I'll show you."

After a stop at the store for the diabetic shakes and snacks, then a smooth trip to the bank, Noel received cash from his deposit. He wouldn't get his debit card until later in the mail.

"Feel good to have some money in the bank?" Justin asked as he drove to the tree lot.

"Yeah, it's starting to feel real now."

"What do you mean?"

"I'm starting to pull pieces of my life back together again."

"I figure it'll take you time to settle in and get comfortable. You don't need to look over your shoulder, wonder when things will drop."

Noel stared at the falling snow. "Yeah, it isn't a fun feeling."

"I'm still trying to figure out how you could deal with something of that magnitude with such poise and you're not bitter and angry," Justin said.

"One day at a time to survive, find a meal, figure out where to sleep, and do it all over again in the morning. If you let everything overcome you, the process can be overwhelming. I kept moving, found ways to stay occupied, upbeat. Bitter and angry don't serve any purpose other than to drag you down further."

"Then you found your way to my small town."

"Yeah, guess it was a good thing I got left behind in Wilmington and found this place on a map."

"I'm happy the bus left you behind too," Justin said and pulled into a parking place. "Here's the tree lot. This is my favorite place to find a tree every year. Are you ready to find a tree with me?"

"I've never done this before," Noel admitted.

"I had a feeling you hadn't." Justin fingered the card Noel had left on his lap to draw his attention to the calligraphy note. "I wanted to show you everything fun and beautiful with the holiday. This is one of them. You can't screw this up. I promise."

After Noel put the card in his bag, Justin got out and waited for Noel to exit. He joined their hands together and walked to the lot. They gazed at and studied the evergreens, lit by the lights and covered with a soft covering of snowflakes, which continued to fall.

"Stand here for a moment. Smell the wonderful, crisp scents of fir, pine, and balsam. They are some of my favorite scents of the season." Justin moved to stand behind Noel, he let go of Noel's hand and placed his hands on Noel's hips. "Just breathe it in."

Noel held still against him, but Justin could hear the deep even breathing.

"What do you think?"

Noel reached a hand to one tree and ran his fingers over the fragrant evergreen needles. "They're wonderful."

"Hello, folks. Looking for a fine Christmas tree for your home this evening?" a fellow asked as he walked over to them, dressed in a cheery red and green apron with the farm's logo embroidered on the front.

"We are. I need one between five and six feet and no bald spots. I prefer lots of fragrance with my tree," Justin said as he stepped to Noel's side and took his hand again.

"Then I would suggest one of two types for you, good sir. Come with me over here," the man said with a wide smile.

"Ahh, good man."

"One question for you on scent. Pine or balsam?" The man stopped in another aisle and turned to face them as he pulled on a pair of work gloves.

Justin looked to Noel. "Which would you prefer?"

"I don't know the difference," Noel said in a sheepish tone.

"Let me give you a sniff test," the man said with a chuckle. "Here is one of our favorites, a gorgeous white pine we cultivate on our farm." He pulled a healthy six-foot tree from a stack, stood it straight, and let it bounce to show no needles fell off the branches. "The branches are nice and full, the needles soft and easy to hang ornaments from. This beauty will give you a strong pine fragrance throughout the season."

Both Justin and Noel leaned in to breathe the healthy pine scent from the long, bright green needles clustered in groups of five along the branches.

"Hmm, it's beautiful," Noel said as he feathered his fingers over the needles.

Justin nodded. "What about the balsam?"

"Ahh, another fine tree with a different look and smell," the man said as he set the pine aside and plucked another six-foot tree from a different pile. "This gorgeous beauty is a balsam fir—also grown on our farm."

Again, they leaned in together to breathe in the different scent. Noel lingered a little longer over the deeper green needles.

Justin watched Noel as he considered the trees and scents. He liked seeing the array of emotions cross his expressive face. "Which one do you like better?"

Noel touched the balsam needles and then the white pine needles. He pointed to the white pine and smiled at Justin. "The pine is the winner. I think it smells more like the holiday. Let's go with this one."

"I agree." Justin looked to the man. "We'll take the white pine."

"Good choice. I'll follow you to the front where we'll net and tie her to your car," the man said as he put back the fir tree. He hefted the pine tree to his shoulder and followed them to the front of the lot.

Within a few minutes, their tree had a fresh-cut bottom and was netted to protect its branches. Justin paid for the tree and a bag of fresh clippings. He flipped the backseats in his Soul down and managed to place the tree in the back. He secured it from rolling with the cargo netting.

"I don't know if this will fit," Noel said.

"Did the same thing last year," he said, stepped back while he brushed his hands together. He hit a button on the door and watched the trunk close without hitting the tree. "Sweet! See, I knew it'd fit."

Noel shook his head and chuckled.

Justin turned to shake hands with the lot man. "Thanks so much."

"Have a good Christmas!" the man said.

"We will. Same to you and your family," Justin said as they got into the car and drove away from the lot.

They both breathed in the fresh pine scent.

"We're going to smell this tree for weeks." Justin chuckled as he glanced in the mirror to check out their tree. "I'm going to find needles back there for months. No matter all the trouble fresh ones bring, I can't bring myself to purchase a fake tree. There is something special about having a live Christmas tree. How did you enjoy this part of your Secret Santa card?"

"This is a first time for me, so, yeah, I loved every moment. This part?" Noel's words stopped short as he twisted to stare at Justin. "Wait, you mean there is more?"

"Of course there is more. It doesn't end with the tree. The card did mention 'scents'— plural."

"Oh. I don't know what there is to doing all this Christmas stuff."

"Where did you grow up they wouldn't put up a tree or celebrate the holidays?"

"For the longest time, I lived at a state funded boys home." Noel tapped his fingers on the window. "We had a fake tree with homemade, donated, or hand-me-down ornaments. The house mother and volunteers tried to give us some gifts, but it wasn't much."

"It sounds like they tried."

"It wasn't for our benefit. They put us on display for the community to show how well they treated the poor orphans around the holidays. The youngest kids got the gifts and photographed by the reports, so the home appeared generous. The older kids were held back, kept out of sight."

"What? How could they be so cruel?"

"It's how they ran the house. After a while, I didn't care." Noel tapped his fingernails harder against the window. "I was happy if I got my stomach full."

"Did they acknowledge your birthday?"

"No, too many boys and too little money to waste on frivolous things."

Justin pressed his lips together as his hands tightened around the steering wheel.

"Sorry. Didn't mean to mess up the night," Noel said and fell silent.

Justin couldn't believe what those people did to break the hearts of kids. On the way home, he stopped at the Italian restaurant and picked up dinner for them, keeping within the requirements for Noel's diabetes.

After parking in front of the garage and hitting the clicker to open the main door, Justin unlocked the trunk and got out after turning off the engine. He tossed the keys to Noel. "Go and unlock the front door, not the one to the kitchen. We'll take the tree straight through the foyer and into the living room."

"Do you need me to help carry it?"

"Yup, so get your cute behind back here."

With a roll of his eyes, Noel grabbed all of the bags—grocery, Italian dinner, and his battered messenger. He adjusted them in his hands and flipped through the large ring of keys until he found the right one, and trotted across the porch to the door.

As he watched Noel walk away, Justin let out a long breath and knew what he was doing with the cards was the right thing after listening to Noel talk about his childhood. He needed to make sure this weekend and Christmas rocked beyond anything Noel would ever expect. How could anyone treat children in such a fashion during Christmas? He couldn't understand it. If things did work out between him and Noel, he would help Noel set up any kind of foundation he wanted to help safe-haven babies.

Justin unlatched the cargo netting and grabbed hold of the tree's net with both hands. He tugged and pulled until the tree slid against the liner. "Come on, Mr. Christmas Tree. Out you come," he grumbled.

"You're arguing with a tree. An inanimate object that can't reply back to you," Noel said as he stood next to him. "Unless some critter crawled inside and chatters back. If that happens, I'll haul my ass to the house and let you deal with the furry monster."

"*Shad up!*"

Noel chuckled, leaned over and helped Justin pull the last foot or so until gravity helped take over. The tree tilted and the heavier base dropped and slid to the ground. They got the top out with ease and Justin let the trunk door close. Noel set the alarm.

"You're younger, so you get the heavy end." Justin took hold of the front and middle.

"Hey! This is your tree!" Noel protested.

Justin stuck his tongue out. "Pick it up, pipsqueak."

"Sheesh. Slave labor."

"You'll get a reward."

"Better be something decent."

"Mebbe. At least, you'll find another red envelope in the morning."

With a playful groan, Noel bent, wrapped his arms around the base, and lifted the pine off the ground. "I like my envelopes. Move it, old man."

"Old? Who are you calling old?" Justin sputtered as he led the way into the waiting house. "I should make you get on your hands and knees to secure the base in the stand."

"Secure the base in the stand? What the hell?"

Justin glanced over his shoulder. "Such a newbie. I'm gonna have such fun with you."

Noel narrowed his eyes. "Keep an eye on where you're going or you will be doing a face plant."

Justin turned in time to stop an untimely disaster. "Oops!" He managed to negotiate the stairs without tripping over his feet and dropping the tree.

They entered the house and turned into the living room.

"Okay. We're going to put it in front of the bay window."

"There are chairs blocking the bay window."

"I know. I know. Carry the chairs into the library." Justin adjusted his grip on the tree. "Set it down here against the wall. Go ahead and lock the front door. Take care of the chairs and I'll go to the garage and find the tree stand. Don't cut off the netting, we'll do it after it's in the stand."

Noel held his hands up to placate him. "Not touching a thing. You're in charge."

Justin chuckle, pressed a quick kiss to Noel's cheek, and raced off to the garage. He hit the button to close the outer garage door, turned on the lights, and reached up for the string attached to the attic door. He yanked the door down, caught and unfolded the stairs until they reached the ground. Then he stared at the black rectangle opening surrounded by the white ceiling. "I hate going up there."

"Are you okay?" Noel called.

"Come to the garage and keep an eye out for me," Justin yelled back through the open interior door. "Make sure I don't fall on my ass." He heard Noel's jogging steps across the wood and tile before he appeared in the doorway.

"Wouldn't be a good thing to have you fall on your behind, since I have no clue what you're about to do up there." Noel pressed his hands on the frame. He shifted a foot to prevent a curious Marlowe from escaping into the garage.

"Marlowe! Don't even think about it," Justin warned the cat.

A stubborn meow left the feline.

"You better come in and close the door on him," Justin said. "If he comes in here, we'll lose him for hours. I'm sure Raleigh is close behind him."

Noel shifted the feline back with his shoe and closed the door before the cat could get through. They heard Marlowe's plaintive meows. A furry gray paw appeared and disappeared under the door.

Noel stared at the paw in curiosity. "Can he pop open the door?"

"He'll try his best, but no."

A different pitched meow sounded. A white paw joined the gray one.

"What about now?"

Justin glanced at the fluffy paws and sighed. "Crazy cats. We need to keep an eye on them and the tree."

"Don't tell me. They like to climb it."

"Yes, well, Marlowe is the climber and will knock the ornaments off."

Noel laughed. "That is one crazy cat."

"That's my furry boy."

"What about Raleigh?"

"He's just as bad. Don't let his grumpy nonchalant attitude fool you. Raleigh will sit and bat at the ornaments and nibble on the needles, but he won't climb." Justin went to the workbench and grabbed the chargeable flashlight from the wall-holder. He clicked the button to test it and luckily, it still worked. He tucked the handle in a back pocket and climbed the stairs. "Okay. Going into the deep abyss. Wish me luck."

"I could be a brat and hit the outer garage door and trap you up there, but I won't. Promise. I swear." Noel grinned when Justin bent over to shoot him a nasty glare from the opening. "Do you have any ideas where you stashed things?"

"Shouldn't have moved from where I placed them last year," Justin said.

"Smart ass."

Justin ducked his head down and grinned at Noel. He disappeared back in the opening until only his legs showed.

"Cool act. Come and see the show, folks. Half of a man disappears," Noel said in a sideshow announcer voice.

"Ha. Ha. Ha." Justin moved the flashlight around, talked aloud to himself as he located things by sight, and found them. "Ah-ha! Bright red tubs. Got them! Can you come over and catch while I slide them down the stairs?"

"Sure. How many are we talking about?"

"A dozen or so. I emptied the one which held the outdoor lights."

"Holy moly!"

"What? I have a house."

"Never mind. Start sending them down."

Justin moved further up the stairs, set the flashlight on a different tub. He moved into position, lifted a bright red tub, and held the base against the stairs. He slid it halfway down the stairs until he felt Noel grasp the other side and let go. After he watched Noel set the tub to one side, he repeated the procedure until they had all twelve tubs down and stacked.

Noel brushed his dusty hands together and peered up the ladder. "Are we done?"

Justin looked around with the flashlight. "Yup. I believe I transferred everything last year to those tubs, so I wouldn't lose or forget anything. I wanted everything to finally match and was determined to accomplish it last year. Coming down. We'll move those inside and I'll pull the car in so it doesn't get buried from the storm."

"I'll start moving them. Anything in particular we're looking for?"

"Yeah. One marked *Tree Lights and Stand* is what we need first. Put that one by the tree. Others can get stacked near the free wall."

"Gotcha. I think I saw the one you mean," Noel said and went to the stacked tubs.

A little over ten minutes later, Justin was on his hands and knees, fiddled with the screws on the tree stand, while Noel stood by with the tree.

"What are you doing?" Noel asked, leaning over to watch him.

"I'm opening the screws to make enough room for the base, but I don't want them so loose the tree is wobbly and you need to hold the tree forever while I tighten them. The base can't hit the bottom, there needs to be space below for the water to flow underneath. The tree sucks it up as needed to stay fresh."

"This sounds like more trouble than this tree is worth," Noel said. "We could go the fake route and pine spray."

"Oh, shush." Justin checked his measurements with his hand and fingers. "Okay. Lift and lower the base. Listen to me for directions."

"You got it," Noel said as he grasped the tree and net and lifted both. He moved it over the stand.

"Little more. Little more. Left... Right a smidge. Another smidge. More. Down, down, down..." Justin continued to direct until the base centered. "Okay. Now hold it right there if you can."

"I'll do my best."

Justin twisted the screws two at a time on opposite sides to make sure he kept the tree straight. When the screws made contact, he went to the other screws and spun those until they made contact. He returned to the first set, turned until they bit further into the bark and finished with the last ones. "Okay, Noel. Release the tree."

"You sure?"

"Yup. Go and stand on the other side of the room and tell me if she stands straight." Justin looked away from the stand and saw Noel's shoes moved away from his side until he couldn't see them. "How does it look?"

"A little to the left. This is your left, sorry."

"Got it." Justin adjusted the corresponding screws. "Now?"

"Looks good to me. I'm lining her up against the main frame of the bay window and she matches."

"Perfect." Justin crawled out from under the tree. "Can you grab the scissors from the kitchen? Oh, and get about two cups of water in a measuring cup. Also the bottle of vodka from the lower cabinet next to the pantry."

"Vodka? I don't think the tree can get drunk."

"Smart ass. Vodka helps keep the tree fresh. Better than those packets being sold at the tree stand. Go get the stuff."

With a chuckle, Noel jogged off to the kitchen.

Justin sat on the wooden floor and brushed himself off. He ran fingers through his hair, plucking stray needles bits of resin from his hair. "Ouch..." he muttered when he pulled a small drop and bit of hair. "Dang it."

"What happened?"

Justin held out his hand. "Pine resin from the tree."

Noel shook his head. "Crazy." He held out his offerings. "Bottle of vodka, water, and scissors."

"We'll need to keep it well watered to prevent the needles from drying out. And keep the cats away from it as well." He crawled under the tree and took the measuring cup. After he filled the stand with water, he cracked open the bottle of vodka and added some to the water. He closed the bottle, patted the base, and backed out. He set the bottle and measuring cup on a nearby table. With the scissors, he clipped the net free from the base to the top. Once he unwound the net and stepped back, the branches opened, but didn't completely fall. "She is a beauty. We made a good choice."

"What next? The branches are clumped weird," Noel asked as he tipped his head to study the pine.

"We give the branches time to fall and settle into their natural state overnight. When we get home tomorrow, we'll wrap the lights and a pearl garland. The ornaments will wait for the party. We can put up the other decorations tomorrow too, along with getting the rest of our shopping and cooking done. We're working from seven to two tomorrow and will be off on Sunday."

"Off? Why? I don't mind working. I need..."

"One... I'm the boss and it's my decision. Two... It's part of the red envelopes."

Noel pulled his eyebrows together. "The red envelopes?"

"Ehh." Justin waved a hand between them. "Don't ask, I'm not answering."

"Are you going to leave me hanging?"

"Yup. Ugh, need to shower and change. We'll get some dinner and head to bed. You need to check your blood, right?"

"Yeah, but..." Noel tried.

"Nope, health comes first." Justin leaned over, tugged Noel close by grasping hold of his shirt, and smacked a light kiss on Noel's surprised lips. "Go and take care of yourself."

Noel blinked.

Justin smacked Noel on his ass. "Go."

"Umm... Okay." Noel studied him for a moment, grabbed his messenger bag, and headed upstairs.

Justin grinned as Noel climbed the stairs. He gave Noel a cheeky wave when the younger man bent down on the landing to study him as if he wasn't sure what Justin was doing to him.

Chapter Nine

On the 3ʳᵈ Day of Christmas, My Safe Haven Gave to Me:
A Christmas Season to Believe In!
~ Secret Santa

The next morning, Justin heard Noel's familiar footsteps going down the stairs and across the wood to the tile flooring. A crooked grin crossed his face at the sight of the red envelope dangling from Noel's fingers. His grin widened when Noel pecked a kiss on his cheek. He found himself having the time of his life this Christmas giving Noel these envelopes and gifts before the actual day and seeing the way Noel reacted to each one.

"Good morning, Noel, how are you today? As always you're looking quite spiffy," he asked after Noel's kiss. He placed the breakfast of French toast on the table. "I thought something a little special this morning to start our day." He set a cup of coffee in front of Noel. "Help yourself." He sat and made up his own plate of bacon and French toast, which he covered with dark maple syrup.

"I'm good. The pine scent is strong, even drifting upstairs to the bedroom," Noel said as he added food to his plate. He captured a droplet of syrup on his finger and sucked it into his mouth.

Justin's cock thickened with desire at the sight of Noel's lips wrapped around the digit. He licked his lips and held back a moan.

"Justin?"

"Hmm?"

Noel doctored his coffee and glanced at Justin. "You okay?"

Justin flushed, stuffed some French toast in his mouth, and nodded. "Yup."

Noel waved the card between them. "What is this all about? You're getting more cryptic as we get closer to Christmas."

"Don't want to make things too easy for you to figure out."

"Yeah, well, whatcha mean?"

"Later."

"Ugh. Not again."

Justin winked. "Eat. We're gonna have another crazy day at the store."

Noel let out a frustrated groan, finished eating, and took one of the shakes, along with a few of the diabetic nutrition bars for snacks during the day.

Hours later, the exhausted men laughed as they plopped their sore bodies in Justin's Soul, groaning at any little protest of their muscles. They hadn't even worked an entire day, but damn, Justin didn't think he wanted to see another holiday in his life.

"You sure it is two? Feels like five," Noel murmured from his spot.

"Yeah, it's two."

Noel whimpered.

"Don't worry, the season is over for us. I'm not opening the store tomorrow or Monday. To hell with the sales. I looked at the books and we're fine."

Noel let out another chuckle and groaned. "What next? A nap?" He closed his eyes as if he was about to fall asleep for the ride home.

"Nope. Your card."

Noel cracked open one set of heavy lids. "Huh?"

Justin hit the start button and rubbed his hands together. "It's our turn to shop and enter the madness."

"Oh, hell."

"Hey, hey. You can't knock it until you try it."

"Must I?"

"Yes."

"Where are we going?"

"We're heading away from here to start and work our way home."

Noel whimpered in fear of what they were about to encounter.

Justin laughed even more as he pulled out and entered the fray of holiday shoppers.

The sun was low in the sky by the time they reached the house, both men dog-tired and a little frustrated, but thrilled at all the sales and finds. Laden with numerous bags, they waddled into the house. By mutual decision, they dropped everything filled with gifts in the living room, returned to the car and retrieved the grocery reusable totes.

"Set up dinner for us while I sort out the cold stuff. The pantry crap can wait until we eat," Justin said.

"Sounds good," Noel said as he found dishes and silverware. He grabbed the jug of fresh iced tea and some soy sauce and carried everything to the table.

Justin watched him sit hard in a chair before he opened the Chinese restaurant bag and pulled out the various containers.

"Is this another tradition of yours? Go crazy with shopping and then get take-out?" Noel asked as he opened the containers.

"Yup, by the end of a workday and shopping, I'm too damn exhausted to make something or wait for delivery. Since I'm out already, easier to pick up something. Part of your previous card, another scent of the season," Justin said and teased as he finished putting away the cold grocery items. He pulled out a chair and settled next to Noel. "Ahh, my favorite—Kung Pao Chicken."

"Cashew chicken is mine," Noel said as he wrapped an arm around the container and drew it toward him. He held a fork up to fend off Justin.

Justin chuckled and held his hands up in surrender. "All yours, I promise. Kung Pao is mine." He pulled the container toward him. "We'll share the chicken fried rice and the wonton soup. Fair?"

"Fair." Noel scooped some white rice onto his plate and slid it to Justin. He poured some of the chicken cashew mixture on top. "Ahh, been a while since I could enjoy this. Thank you." He scooped a full forkful and shoveled it into his mouth.

Justin chuckled and nodded. "Welcome." He started to fill his mouth and stomach with dinner.

When they'd finished eating, Noel excused himself after a loud belch.

Justin laughed and sat back while he sipped from another glass of tea. "No problem, glad you enjoyed dinner."

"Oh yeah, my favorite," Noel said while he pushed back the plate. "Better check my sugars."

"Go ahead. I'll clean this mess up, put away the pantry stuff, and we'll start on the decorations."

"Decorations?"

"Did you think we were done for the day?"

"Umm. Yeah."

"We still need to put lights on the tree, fill the rest of the house with decorations, wrap the gifts, and..."

"Justin... Tomorrow? We're not working."

"We have guests coming for a party which means cooking food, baking, and cleaning."

"Yeah, after all the other stuff."

"Come on, there is still time for us to work on the tree and house before bedtime," Justin said.

"This Christmas stuff is a lot of work." Noel yawned as he rose and gathered his things and carried them to the kitchen. He rinsed and placed his dirty plate and silverware in the dishwasher.

"I know it is, but there is such reward in the end." Justin followed with his dishes and set them on the counter. Unable to stop himself, he placed his hand on either side of Noel and leaned in against him. He lowered his head and nuzzled a kiss to the back of Noel's neck. "Please."

"Such a charmer," Noel murmured.

Justin grinned against Noel's skin. He felt he was beginning to break through Noel's walls. When he felt Noel lean a bit, giving him access for more skin to be kissed and touched, Justin took the step offered. He kept his kisses light, flirty, and flicked his tongue against sensitive nerve endings as he worked his way from where the shoulder and neck met to a soft spot under his ear which made Noel moan in a delicious way. Justin pressed a hand against Noel's lower abdomen to bring him back against his body. His lips continued to move against the warm heated skin while Noel raised a hand and his fingers tangled in Justin's hair.

"Please..." Noel whispered. "Justin... Kiss me."

Justin leaned back and met a grayish-blue gaze darkened with arousal and passion as Noel turned his head. He drew his other fingers over the light stubble rising across Noel's lower face, golden against the pale skin and the angles of Noel's chin.

When Noel's mouth opened under his, it was perfect and right as it had been every single time when they kissed. Only this one seemed more passionate than their previous kisses. This time, they knew one another and wanted more. Noel's lips were firm and male and strong under his mouth as they matched his with every movement. Justin slipped his tongue inside to deepen the kiss and Noel responded by lowering his hands to clutch at him.

Justin intensified the kiss. When Noel whimpered against him, he felt the bite of Noel's fingers on his shoulders.

Justin pulled up, brushed their lips together, and saw the flush over Noel's face.

Noel leaned heavily against the counter, almost in a swoon from the passion. His lips were red and kiss-swollen. He slid his tongue against the lower lip and moaned.

The sound was so decadent it almost brought Justin to his knees and a fierce orgasm.

"I want you so much, dream boy, but not yet," Justin admitted as he ran a single finger against those angles and stubble.

"Why not?" Noel dragged his gaze up Justin's body until they met and held.

"I promised I wouldn't take advantage—"

"You're not!"

"Ssh." Justin pressed his fingers against Noel's swollen lips. "I would be."

Noel looked away, his jaw clenched. "I'm not a child or anything. I may need to rely on you for almost everything right now, but it doesn't mean you get to make a decision about my body too." He crossed his arms as he stepped away.

"I didn't mean that to sound horrible to you. Of course I don't look down on you." Justin tried to place a hand on Noel's shoulder, but Noel brushed him off.

Noel moved further away and stalked out of the kitchen. "Perhaps it would be best I start paying you rent or something then. I don't think I should help string the lights. I'm not good company right now."

With a heavy sigh, Justin listened as Noel stormed up the stairs. His plans started to fray and fall apart in his head.

After taking some time to finish cleaning their dinner, putting away the rest of the groceries, and grabbing a cold shower, Justin changed into a pair of sweatpants and a college T-shirt before going downstairs to tackle the tree alone. He didn't hear anything from Noel's room when he passed by both times.

Needing a distraction from the silence, he chose a Christmas playlist from his iPod and placed the player in the dock. He hit the play button to fill the downstairs with the holiday sounds. Then he sat cross-legged in front of the one tub marked "lights" and began the process of untangling the strands.

"Damn lights. Bane of my existence every year," he muttered as he plugged the strand into the surge protector he used for the season. His lap and floor covered with sparkling white lights. "Whoa. Getting hot down there." He pulled a tangle away from his crotch.

When he'd gone through several knots and tangles, Justin stared at the pile and what waited in the tub. "This needs chocolate and cookies." He stopped the process and went to the kitchen to fix some needed hot chocolate with soy milk and marshmallows. He added a plate of chocolate chip cookies he'd saved for this particular night. He carried both back to the living room and stopped.

Noel sat in front of the tree, a string of lights in his lap, his fingers worked out one of the nastier tangles.

"Uhh... Hi," Justin said, not sure what else to say. He felt like a dolt.

"You call this fun?" Noel held up the knot.

"Not this part, no. This is the pain in the ass part to get to the fun."

"Hmm. I smell hot chocolate."

"I made the chocolate with soy, though."

"Umm, it's still chocolate."

Justin set the cup on the table next to Noel. "I'll pour another mug for me. Here are some cookies."

"Is this part of the tradition?"

"I craved some chocolate sustenance against the tangles. They started to win the battle when they almost tried to burn my balls. Not a good feeling." Justin returned to the kitchen and prepared another mug of chocolate fortitude for himself. After a sip, he walked back to the tree and settled down across from Noel.

"Not bad with soy," Noel said with a nod to the mug.

"I've fiddled with the recipe over the years."

"Are you telling me this is homemade? Like with cocoa powder and all that stuff."

"Yup, not as good as Leroy's, but I don't have time to melt chocolate like he does."

"Leroy's is off the charts awesome, but I'm liking this cup. I would just grab a packet and go at it."

"Don't like the packets since most of them are sugar and not chocolate. Besides, I like fresh marshmallows. Sorry, I don't have whip cream for you."

"No, I don't mind. This is great." Noel rolled the cup carefully between his hands. He studied the lights strewn across the floor and his lap. "I'm sorry about earlier. I acted like a child."

"It's okay. If I'm pushing you into doing something too fast, please tell me. Don't storm off and not tell me why. I can't help if I don't know what's wrong."

"Why won't you take me to your bed?"

Justin looked over and waited until Noel met his gaze. "You're trying to get back on your feet and figure out who you are, Noel." He pointed a finger at Noel's heart. "Deep inside there. You'll find yourself."

"Sex has nothing to do with me finding myself."

"It can have everything and ruin a relationship. I don't want to jump into bed with you. It would be meaningless and confuse everything."

"I'm not confused."

"Could you please trust me on this and not run from me?"

Noel tilted his head. Justin could almost see him running the conversation through his head again and picking it apart. "Is there a time frame?"

Justin shook his head. "Nope."

Noel blew out a frustrated breath. "Okay. I'll wait."

"I'm not talking years or even months. Okay?"

Noel nodded and set the mug of hot chocolate aside and picked up the strand of lights. "How many of these are left?"

Justin reached in the tub for another strand and worked on it after plugging it in so the lights could show him where the tangles were. "Hopefully not too many. Depends on how many we have working without dead bulbs. One bulb can screw up an entire strand."

Noel whipped out the last knot with a triumphant sound and set the strand aside. He leaned over the tub and pulled another strand. "This is the last one."

"About damn time we hit the bottom. After that, we plug them end to end and wrap them around the tree."

"I don't see the bottom of the tub. There is a mound of fabric on the bottom. I see three plastic containers with ropes of white beads."

"That would be the tree skirt to wrap around the stand. Ahh, the containers are filled with the pearl garland. We'll do the pearls after we finish the lights."

When they straightened all the strands and stretched out across the wooden floor, Justin instructed Noel to plug in the first strand as he gathered the rest of the length in his hands. He slid in around the tree and wove it around the branches to make the tree glow. Before he came to the end, Noel was there with the next one. They worked as a smooth team to cover the tree, not leaving an empty space. Justin showed Noel how to tuck the wires back in the branches to hide them, but let the tiny bulbs shine.

"When we hang the ornaments tomorrow with the guests, a lot of the lights will backlight them, make them sparkle brightly. It'll be beautiful," Justin said as he adjusted one of his strands and stepped back when they reached the top.

"Got them all?"

"Yup. Now the garland and skirt and the tree will be ready for tomorrow."

Noel went to the tub and pulled out the plastic containers. Inside each container were plastic tubes, each with a single strand of ivory pearl garland. "Hey, these aren't tangled. Sweet!"

"Yeah, I learned to pack them in those tubes to prevent them from twisting on each other." Justin used the twist tie on one end of the garland to secure it to a back branch, then started to make simple swag under and over branches and checked the spacing. Again, before he finished one, Noel handed him another rope so he could secure both and continued to swag.

"Damn, this is a lot of garland," Noel said when they finished the last tube in the third container.

"Yeah, about fifty feet worth, but it makes the tree look real special." Justin secured the last piece and they stepped back to look at their handiwork.

"It is lovely." Noel handed him the skirt.

"Last piece," Justin said as he unfolded the ivory, silver, and midnight blue skirt. "William and his wife gave this to me the year I purchased BookWorm."

"William is married?"

"To a gorgeous lady name Christina. You'll meet her tomorrow. She'll mother you like crazy. It's her nature to take any lonely soul under her wing." Justin gathered the plastic containers, tossed them back in the tub, and closed it. He slid it along the floor toward the kitchen.

"Why did you do that?"

"Get it out of the way. I'll leave them in the garage until it's time to take all this down." Justin rubbed his hands together. "One down, eleven to go. Lemme see which ones are ornaments."

"Stack them by the tree?"

"Yup."

Together they found the ones marked *Ornaments* and separated them from the rest. Justin stacked them on the wall near the tree. There were five total when they'd finished.

"Are we going to use all five?" Noel asked.

"No, not everything goes on the tree, but I end up keeping everything. Sometimes I change the color of the ornaments from one year to the next, depending on my whim or those of the guests. We'll decide tomorrow. The colors are marked on the tubs."

Two tubs were marked *Tins and Kitchen*. Justin slid them to the kitchen along the wooden floor. "What's next?"

"We're down to three for the rest of the house. This seems a little more manageable," Noel said.

"Yup. Other than the tree stuff, I don't go overboard. There's not as much in the tubs as you think because some of it is wrapped to prevent breakage."

"Wanna keep going then?"

Justin opened the three lids. "How about we lay out everything on the dining table? Then tomorrow, we can pull down the everyday decorations, put them in the tubs for storage, and set up the Christmas stuff in between the baking and cooking."

"I'm following your plan and lead."

Justin rubbed a hand over Noel's shoulder. "I want to make this a good Christmas season for you, not overwhelm you."

"If it's like this all the time, then I want to get a taste of everything." Noel tugged one of the tubs to the table and unwrapped each item.

"Oh, it can be much worse. Believe me."

"Don't know if I want to see worse."

Justin gave him an evil grin as they continued to work on emptying the tubs until they decided it was time to call it quits for the evening.

Chapter Ten

On the 2nd Day of Christmas, My One Hope Gave to Me:
Surprises of the Season!
~ Secret Santa

Noel stared at the writing as he fell on the bed. *One hope? What happened to Safe Haven? Surprises? What surprises?* He read and re-read the message.

"I swear he is getting more cryptic with each one of these," Noel told Marlowe.

Marlowe lifted a paw and licked the gray fur.

"And that's what I get for talking to a feline," Noel mumbled as he rose and went through his regular morning testing and routines. Since they weren't going to the store, he changed into jeans and a sweatshirt. He grabbed a pair of warm socks and slipped them over his bare feet. On his way past the bed, he snatched the card and headed downstairs with Marlowe. He noticed picture frames and decorative items were missing from their usual places on the walls and realized Justin had gotten a head start this morning.

"Justin?"

"Kitchen, getting a refill," Justin called back. "Is Marlowe with you?"

"Yeah, he's by my feet."

"Ahh, I figured that since he didn't come down for breakfast with Raleigh. I think I'm getting jealous. My cat likes you more than me."

Noel chuckled at Justin's grumbling tone. He saw items were gone in the kitchen and the tubs emptied on the island. "You've been busy," he said, kissed Justin on the cheek, and headed to the coffee machine for his morning cup. Marlowe moseyed over to his bowl of kibble.

"I couldn't sleep so I got an early start." Justin leaned back against the counter. "I left a plate with an omelet and bacon in the microwave for you. You need to warm it up."

"Oh, thanks. You don't always need to cook for me. I should learn to do something around here," Noel said while he hit the buttons on the microwave to start the process.

"I enjoy cooking and it pleases me to do it for more than one." Justin sipped from his mug as he looked around the messy kitchen. "The entire takedown is done. I gave everything a good dusting while I was at it."

Noel removed his plate from the microwave, grabbed a fork and his mug, and headed to the table to eat. "I don't know where you'd want everything stored. I would've been asking questions left and right, slowing you down." He waved the card. "You changed the wording."

Justin glanced away, but gave no answer.

"Justin..." Noel rose and sauntered over to where he stood. He lifted a hand, pressed his fingers against Justin's cheek, and pivoted until their gazes met. "Why did you put down 'My One Hope'?"

"Can I request not to answer until all the cards are given?"

"When will I receive the last card?"

"Christmas morning."

"You want me to wait until then?"

"Please. You'll understand when you receive all the cards."

Noel dropped his forehead to Justin's shoulders. "Why are you doing this for me?"

"To show you there is another way to love Christmas and the season. To give you a safe haven against the dark side of your life and hope for a brighter future." Justin tilted his head until Noel felt him lean against him. "Perhaps break down the wall guarding your heart."

"I have no idea how to do everything you're asking of me."

"After some time and thought, I hope you'll begin to understand the meaning behind the cards."

"I'm sure you know you're asking for a whole lot of trust from me with these things."

"You've trusted me this far." Justin tilted Noel's face up from his shoulder. A wry grin was on his face.

"Yeah, you're right. Okay. I'll wait."

"Thank you. Finish eating your breakfast. We have a lot to do before our guests arrive."

Noel nodded and turned to move back to his seat.

"Oh, Noel," Justin said.

Noel stopped and looked at him.

Justin cupped Noel's cheeks with his hands. He leaned in and pressed their lips together in a slow, tender kiss. "Happy birthday, dream boy."

Noel flushed under the warm green gaze, filled with hope and care. He recognized all of it was for him. "Thank you."

"Eat. We're on a tight schedule," Justin said as he smack Noel's ass.

"Hey!"

"One for the birthday boy," Justin called as he grabbed his coffee mug and headed out of the kitchen.

Noel rubbed the offended butt cheek. He ate his breakfast, grumbling about the swat. After he'd finished and put the dishes in the dishwasher, he went to find Justin, a mug of coffee in his hands.

"Decided to join me?" Justin lifted his gaze from the various decorations.

"Yeah, guess I better."

"Good. Take this garland and wrap it around the railing. Start at the top, secure it with the twist tie, and go down to the bottom. You'll follow it with the lights and pearl garland like the tree. We'll finish with bows." Justin pointed to a pile of green at the end of the table.

Noel set the mug down, studied the pile, and poked at it with a finger. "What is this?"

"Fake pine garland since you can't find real ones. You can take branches from the bag I got from the tree lot and stick it between some of the loops to carry the scent over there."

"You want me to wrap it around the railing?"

"You go in between the spindles, yes."

With a shrug, Noel gathered the pine branches in his hands and climbed the stairs. He saw the hidden nail to secure the twist tie, and started to work the bendable garland around the wooden railing. He nodded to Justin when he handed over the lights, then the ivory pearls to wind around the pine branches. Noel added some branches from the tree lot bag to the railing decoration.

Justin attached more garland, lights, and pearls to the fireplace mantel. They also set candles in the candlesticks and switched them to a different arrangement. Justin added an arrangement of holly and snowmen to the bases. The rest of the morning passed while they continued to decorate the living room, dining room, front hallway, and staircase. Justin closed off the office, library, and upstairs during the party.

At times, Justin disappeared into the kitchen. Delicious smells wafted from that end of the house as Justin appeared in a dark green apron.

Noel snorted at the hilarious image on the front. It was a cartoon snowman with a large carrot sticking out of the lower ball. He cracked up laughing. "Naughty snowman you got there."

"Yup, I love my snowman. Got another one with a guy sliding backward down a banister called 'the Nutcracker,'" Justin said with a grin.

"Ouch!"

Justin chuckled.

"What are you baking in there?"

"I'm starting to bake cookies. We'll do the sugar cookies together. I have the batter chilling now. We get to roll it out, cut shapes with various Christmas cutters I've gathered over the years, choose sprinkles, and bake. The ones in there now are simple drop cookies—nothing to them. Two Crock-Pots started this morning—one has my infamous smoky fish chowder and the second are two balsamic-glazed pork tenderloins. Both recipes are classics with the party gang who swing in for this shindig."

"Wow. A lot of food."

"A lot of people are coming and they're all coming with an appetite. I also have two Tuscan herb chicken breasts to roast in the upper oven, along with various side dishes. We'll set everything in a buffet style on the sideboard."

"Does it all fit?"

"Yup. I have chafing dishes to keep it all warm too. They're in the tubs and down here," Justin said as he tapped his fingers against the cabinets by the cleaned sideboard where he stood.

"Is that why you put this long fabric thing and candle stuff in the middle of the table?"

"It's called a runner and yes, that's why," Justin said.

"Runner?"

"The fabric thing down the middle of the table is called a runner."

"Oh." Noel surveyed the room and the stacked tubs filled with the everyday decorations. "It looks like everything is in its place. Want me to put the tubs in the garage?"

A timer dinged to alert Justin.

"Please, that would be wonderful. I need to switch out the trays of cookies," Justin said as he rushed back to the kitchen.

"No problem," Noel said as he returned to work.

After his testing and a simple lunch, Noel helped Justin finished the sugar cookies. He sampled some of the earlier treats to his delight.

"Oh, did you finish wrapping your gifts?" Justin asked as he slid the cookies onto one of the prepared sheets.

"No, I didn't. I need to before everyone arrives."

"Yeah. I did the ones for the party last night. Let me get you the scissors, paper, and tape from my room. Hang on. If this beeps before I get back, slide the tray onto the middle rack. Use the mitt to protect your hand. Set the timer for ten minutes. Okay?"

Noel nodded.

Kissing Noel's cheek, Justin left him alone in the kitchen to retrieve the items. Sure enough, the oven dinged with the readied temperature.

"I can do this. It's easy." Noel slid the mitt on his hand, opened the door, grabbed the sheet of cookies, and placed the tray on the rack where he'd watched Justin put all the others. He closed the door and set the timer.

"Hey, you did it. Congrats on baking your first sheet of cookies." Justin entered with a tall container of wrapping material.

"Easy enough to handle..." Noel gave the container a wary gaze. "This now, I'm not too sure about. I've never wrapped a gift before, let alone given one. How about I put them all in gift bags?"

"How about this? Bring down everyone's but the ones you got for me. I'll help you with those, then you can wrap mine upstairs so you can keep those a secret. We'll do it at the far end of the table so the paper and gifts don't get dirty."

Noel turned to study the table and shrugged. "Okay. Let me get them."

Within a few moments, Noel had his gifts spread about on one end of the table, each one still in the bag from the store. He put the name of each recipient on a sticky note next to the item so he wouldn't forget who got what.

After Justin switched out the cookie sheets in the oven, slid the finished cookies to a cooling rack, he sat next to Noel. "Wow. These are gorgeous gifts. You did wonderful for your first time out."

"You helped a lot." Noel ran a hand over his short hair. "I hate not knowing how to do all this. I mean... I'm twenty-two. I should know how to shop for people, wrap a stupid gift, decorate a house, or bake cookies, but I don't. I know nothing."

"Hey. Hey, ssh, none of this is your fault," Justin said as he slid his chair over and wrapped his arms around Noel. Then he tugged him over for a soothing, comforting hug.

Noel buried his face against Justin's chest as he released the tears held for far too long. He felt Justin's fingers tangle and play in his hair. His fingers clutched at the silly apron.

They stayed in each other's arms until the ding of the timer forced them to break away. With a murmured apology, Justin unfolded and went to the oven. After he slid in the final batch, he returned to the table where Noel had taken the brief time to compose himself.

"Are you okay?"

"Yeah," Noel said as he gripped Justin's hand with his fingers. "Show me how to wrap these so I can put them under the tree."

"Let's start with the easy ones that don't need a box or anything." Justin reached for one. "Choose a paper from the container. I opened some already so you may want to use different ones for yours."

Together, they laughed and joked as Noel learned how to wrap Christmas gifts. The results weren't neat or perfect, but they were pretty with ribbon finishes and curls and a tag written in Noel's hand. Interspersed with wrapping, Justin worked in the kitchen on the various dishes and treats.

The cats kept wandering in the kitchen, meowing at all the scents, and demanding treats. They kept getting pushed back out from their feline demands by a patient Justin.

After Noel signed the last tag, he stacked the gifts and carried them to the tree. He placed them around the base in a neat pile. He returned to the kitchen and gathered what he needed to wrap the last of the gifts upstairs. "I'm going upstairs to finish. Okay?"

"Sure. Watch out for the ribbon and Marlowe. You can dangle a piece with him, but don't leave him alone with it. He can choke on it."

"I'll remember," Noel said. "Sorry, I can't help with all the food stuff."

"Eh! I got this all covered. This is one of my favorite parts. You can help me set everything up in an hour or so. Okay?"

"Sure. Be back in a bit." Noel went upstairs.

"Might as well go change into a party outfit while you're up there. Not much time left," Justin called after him.

Noel groaned.

Hours later, a holiday cocktail in his hand, Noel found himself mingling with the large crowd in Justin's home. Christmas music played from the docked iPod, loud enough to hear but not overpower everyone's conversations. Everyone enjoyed the appetizers and cocktails.

The tree was a main focal point, lit and ready for the ornaments while everyone voted on this year's color scheme during cocktails. Justin set out the different color sets on three trays and a stack of paper, pens, and a basket with a lid to hold the votes on a table near the tree. The guests were to pick their favorite color, write it down, and add it to the basket. Justin would count the votes after they ate dinner and they would decorate before opening gifts, having cookies and coffee and playing games.

Noel lifted his drink and spun as kids raced passed him, chasing one another through the crowd. He blinked at their speed. He took a sip of the drink, felt a little uneasy at the crowds. He turned his head when he felt a warm arm slide around his waist.

Justin smiled at him and pressed a kiss to his cheek. "I didn't tell you earlier, dream boy, but you look gorgeous in your outfit. The blue sweater sets off your eyes."

Noel flushed.

Justin offered him goodies from a plate. "Here. Balance out the alcohol you're drinking."

"I don't know if I can—" Noel waved the glass toward the crowd of people. "At the store, it's different. It's anonymous and I'm working. It's a job. Here…"

"Things are more personal and you don't have the job to hide behind. I know, dream boy." Justin moved his hand from Noel's waist and slid his fingers through Noel's hair. "You're doing okay. You can handle this. I would like you to switch to iced tea, though. You've had one too many drinks tonight."

Noel glanced at the empty glass, his third of the night, and wavered. "Yeah. Think so too. Not good, but needed some courage."

"Here, eat some of this. I'll make another plate. Sit here and I'll be right back with a glass of tea and my plate." Justin helped him over to a chair and sat him down. He put the plate on his lap, took the glass, and disappeared in the crowd.

He nibbled a few bites when Justin returned and perched on the arm while he balanced a plate on his lap. Justin set two glasses of iced tea on the mantel behind them. Justin caressed his cheek with the back of his fingers and lifted his gaze to meet his.

"How are you? You doing okay? Having fun?" Justin asked.

"Yeah, I'm having fun. I like meeting everyone, just not all at once. A little overwhelming, but I'm okay. Promise," Noel said as he popped another appetizer in his mouth. A few chomps and he swallowed with a grin. "These are delicious."

"Thank you. I love cooking for everyone."

"Hey there, you two. Food is delicious as always, Justin," William said as he broke through the crowd. A petite silver-haired lady in a black and silver dress followed him.

"William, there you are. I didn't see you come in," Justin said as he rose and gave the older man a one-arm hug. "Mama Christina! Sweetheart, when are you going to leave this old goat and disappear with me?" He scooped her into his hug.

"You silly rogue," the lady said with a laugh as she hugged him back and kissed his cheek. "How are you, my sweet boy? You're looking fine tonight."

"Ahh, you know me. I'm in my element," Justin said as Christina checked him out.

Noel watched everything from his seat, a little uncomfortable with the closeness between the trio. Once again, he felt like an outcast.

"Mama Christina, I found another lost bird for you to take under your wing. He's been staying with me." He pivoted the couple to face Noel, who rose, set the plate on his seat, and wiped his fingers on a napkin. "Christina Bonnaire, I would like you to meet Noel Hudson. Noel, this is Christina, William's much better and prettier half," Justin introduced.

"Hey!" William punched Justin in the shoulder.

"Boys!" Christina smacked both of them in their stomachs and stepped closer to embrace Noel, who remained a little stiff. "Hello, Noel, what a wonderful pleasure to meet you. I've heard much about you from both those crazy nuts."

At the gentleness, warmth, and softness of the older woman's embrace, Noel relaxed and hugged the woman. He thought Justin was right when he said Christina was motherly.

Christina stepped back, placed a light touch on Noel's cheek, and he flushed under her careful gaze. "Are you fattening this beautiful boy with your good food, Justin?"

"We're working on it." Justin moved around and slid an arm around Noel's waist.

"I have diabetes, so things are a little hard to control. I need to figure out why my blood sugars aren't where they need to be," Noel admitted.

"Oh dear, well, I can help you there, sweet one," Christina said.

Noel pulled his eyebrows together in confusion.

"I'm a nurse in a free clinic. I see diabetic clients all the time. We'll check things out after dinner. They'll be busy counting those silly votes. You'll be back before they start to decorate the tree."

"You don't mind helping me?"

"Not at all, sweetie. I'll send William out in the snow to get my bag. I carry it with me all the time. He's used to it."

"Thank you. I would feel better and I know Justin would too," Noel said and felt Justin give him a squeeze.

"Good. It's a plan then." Christina turned to William. "Appetizers and cocktails, darling. I'm starving."

"Yes, dear," William said as her ever-devoted slave. "Usual place, Justin?"

"Yup. Whole assortment is there," Justin said.

Noel and Justin chuckled as the couple disappeared in the crowds.

"You're right, she is wonderful," Noel said as he picked up the plate and sat.

"Yeah. Christina is the best. Though I had my grandmother, Christina is there for me no matter what," Justin said as he settled next to Noel.

They continued to nibble on appetizers, chat with guests, and enjoy the party.

Chapter Eleven

"What's the verdict?" Noel asked as he tugged on his sweater and sat on the edge of his bed. He petted a purring Marlowe's soft fur. Both of the cats hid in his room during the party, but Raleigh mewled under the bed. He watched Christina jot a few notes in a new folder she'd created for Noel's history.

"Your blood sugar levels are rocky from what you showed me in the diary. I'm afraid you could slip into diabetic ketoacidosis if we don't figure out the correct amount of insulin. You know the symptoms to look out for with this illness, correct?" Christina asked while she put her things in a backpack.

"Yeah, I know to seek emergency help if my blood sugar levels stay consistently higher than three hundred, excessive thirst or pee, nausea and vomiting," he said and listed the rest of the symptoms with care and precision. "I went through it once and ended up in a hospital. Not a fun ordeal."

"No, it isn't and can be deadly." She checked his numbers. "You're running higher than I'd like. Let's increase every evening for a week, keep a record of your numbers and diet. Try to keep to the digestible diet of salt, carbs, and foods low in sugars. I'll return and we'll check you again. Any issues, you call me right away." She gave him a card.

Noel took the business card and double-checked the numbers. "Okay. I can do all this. If not, I'm sure Justin will kick my ass if I forget."

"Do you have enough supplies?"

"I'm running low, actually. I mentioned to Justin I need to find a way to replenish them. Since I'm not a registered patient or anything here, I didn't know where to go for supplies." He told her how much he had left when she asked.

"Okay, I'll add you to our supply list and you should get a delivery at the end of the week. If not, call me and we'll get things sorted out before you run out. Is Justin getting you coverage under the store?"

"He said he's working on something."

"Then that's what he's doing. Either way, we'll get you your supplies."

Noel dragged the card along the quilt and played with Marlowe's fur.

"What is it?"

"He's doing everything for me and I..."

"Haven't given him anything in return?"

"I feel horrible, like I'm taking advantage of him."

"You're giving back, Noel, and definitely not taking advantage. Ever since he was a boy, Justin's been alone. I've never seen him so happy and I know it's because of your presence. William mentioned the same thing. He saw it happening weeks ago, when a certain mysterious young man started to sit and read in the store."

Noel flushed. "I needed to get out of the cold. His store was warm and inviting. And he is..."

"Cute, irresistible, and adorable?"

Noel felt his face heat even more.

"I knew the attraction was there." Christina pressed a hand to Noel's heated face. "Don't run from the attraction because you believe you aren't worthy or he's somehow unattainable. Justin would never turn away from you for such a ridiculous reason. He sees your heart, not your circumstances or past."

A knock on the door stopped Noel from replying.

"Come in," Christina called.

The door opened and Justin popped his head around. "Hello. How is my dream boy?"

"We're going to get things under control. Aren't we, Noel?"

Noel nodded as he rose from the bed. "Yeah, we're good."

"Wonderful. We're ready to decorate. The colors are red, midnight blue, and silver this year." Justin held his hand out for Noel to take it. "I wanted you to be the one to put the first ornament on the tree. Everyone is waiting for us to begin."

"Me? Why?"

"Tradition, you're the newcomer to our group and my special guest so you get the first ornament."

"Oh, Justin, I don't know..."

"Please?"

Noel swallowed hard.

"Please?"

Noel saw the pleading adorable look in Justin's gaze and his resistance disappeared. He couldn't say no.

"You can do this," Christina said as she placed her hands on Noel's shoulders.

"We'll be right by your side," Justin promised.

"Okay." Noel placed his hand in Justin's, threaded their fingers together, and they left the room.

When they reached the stairs, Justin nuzzled Noel's neck and whispered, "Remember the card this morning?"

"Yes..." Noel said and noticed the lights dimmed.

"Surprise! Happy Birthday!" everyone shouted when they hit the landing.

Noel's eyelids popped open with shock as his jaw dropped when all the guests broke into the Happy Birthday song for him. William and Jamie carried a tray between them with a huge cake in the shape of a book with his name on top.

"Holy crap!" Noel said, his hands slamming against his mouth, his eyes watering.

Justin laughed at his response and led him down the last two steps to the birthday cake.

"Justin! How? I don't understand..." Noel tried to spit out the words but couldn't.

"A whole lot of behind-the-scenes texting with William and Jamie to get this one accomplished. Did you think I was going to let this birthday go by for you and do nothing?"

Noel shrugged. "I don't care about this day. It means nothing to me. You said there wouldn't be a party for me."

"It *should* mean something. This day will be special for you. I'm sorry I lied a little, but it's for a good cause." Justin caressed Noel's face. "Happy birthday, my dream boy. Make a wish and blow out your candles."

Tears fell from Noel's eyes, but he couldn't wipe them away, not this time. "What would I wish for? You've been granting all of them and ones I haven't even thought of."

"I'm sure you have another one." Justin placed a gentle kiss on his cheek.

Noel closed his eyes and thought of one wish, one more thing to complete his life. *I wish to be Justin's forever — heart, soul, and body.* Leaning over, he opened his eyes and blew out the candles.

Everyone applauded and cheered. Whistles galore erupted when Justin captured him in a heated kiss and embrace.

William, Jamie, and Christina carried the cake to the dining table. Justin and Noel followed so Noel could make the first slice, which he did. He took a thin slice and shared the delicious mocha chocolate with raspberry filling cake with Justin.

"Okay. Start with this ornament. Everyone can add ornaments while they eat their cake and chat," Justin said, handing Noel a delicate blue and silver book.

"This is gorgeous."

"Read the inscription."

Noel lifted the book closer.

Noel

Our 1ˢᵗ Christmas & Many More
Justin

"Oh... It's... I..." Noel swallowed.

"Ssh," Justin said, placed his fingertips on Noel's lips. "Go and hang it on the tree. We'll talk tonight."

Noel pressed a kiss to Justin's fingers, rose to his feet, and went to hang the beautiful book in a prominent position on the tree. He made sure a few lights made the shiny silver glisten and sparkle. He turned to see if Justin approved the spot and saw him nod. He returned to his seat and curled next to Justin's side as others meandered over to hang various balls, stars, crystals, and other doodads Justin had collected, found, or received over the years.

"I love the book. Thank you," Noel said.

"I'm pleased you do. Not mad about the whole surprise twist?" Justin waved his hand to encompass the birthday party.

"I'm in shock about everything. No one has ever thrown me a surprise party. Let alone any kind of party."

"I can find plenty of ways to shock and surprise you."

"I know you can."

Hanging their chosen baubles for the tree, William and Christina stepped over to them with a large wrapped gift. "Happy birthday, Noel. A gift from us, separate from your Christmas gift." William placed it on Noel's lap.

"Happy birthday, sweet boy, and many more," Christina said with a kiss on his cheek.

"What? Oh, you didn't... I..." Noel flushed while he studied the birthday wrapping on the gift.

"We know we didn't have to do anything for your birthday, but how could any of us pass up an opportunity to spoil you rotten, sweet boy?" Christina stepped away with William.

Jamie appeared with another gift. "Happy birthday and here's a little something from my girlfriend, Annie, and me. Oh, sorry, this is Annie. Annie, this is Noel." He introduced the cute redhead.

"Hi, Noel, a pleasure to meet you and happy birthday," the redhead said.

"Hi, Annie, wonderful to meet you as well," Noel replied. He accepted the gift from Jamie. "Thank you both for this."

Soon almost everyone dropped a gift at his feet, wrapped in birthday paper, and wished him birthday greetings. Most he recognized from his single week at the store, but he didn't know them well enough for them to give him gifts.

Tears filled his eyes at their wonderful generosity toward him and he pressed his face into Justin's shoulder. Justin embraced him with one arm around his shoulders. He knew this small town accepted him as one of them, like Justin had welcomed him into his home.

"I found a safe haven," he whispered against Justin.

"Yes, you did, dream boy, you did, and I'm happy you wandered into my store," Justin said and nuzzled a kiss into Noel's hair.

"Everyone, I believe Noel is a little overwhelmed. Is it okay if he opens the gifts once everyone leaves? He can send us a thank-you note. I for one know Justin has plenty of those hidden somewhere in his home," Christina called as she rested her hands on Noel and Justin's backs.

Soft murmurs of approval rose from the crowd.

"Wonderful! Begin the Christmas gift exchange! William, Jamie, will you two play Santa this year?" Christina requested as she took over control of the party. "By the way, everyone, the tree looks fabulous. A round of applause!"

Loud applause thundered as William and Jamie moved to the tree, put on the red Santa hats, and started to pick up wrapped gifts from towering piles. People gathered around the tree, sat to await their gifts in excited anticipation and listen for their names. When the recipient raised their hands, the Santas delivered the package.

Christina and Annie carried in the trays of cookies and hot chocolate with bowls filled with peppermint sticks, marshmallows, and whipped cream. Annie set hers on the dining table where others sat. Christina placed hers on the coffee table. Justin made up a cup with cream and marshmallow and placed it in Noel's hands. Christina sat on a nearby chair.

"Thank you for earlier," Noel whispered to her.

"You're welcome, sweetie. I could tell things were getting a little much halfway through the line. Justin, those mugs are soy milk hot cocoa."

Justin topped his mug with marshmallows and sipped. "Ahh. Bless you, darling." He raised his hand when Jamie called his name.

"I know who you are, nitwit," Jamie said with a snicker as he placed a package on his lap.

"Then why call it out?"

"Tradition," Jamie shot back and returned to the tree.

"Crazy fool," Justin murmured as he checked the tag. "Hmm. One of our Addicts gave this to me."

"Umm. Justin," Noel said while he put his hand up again. He already had six packages on his lap. "I didn't get this many gifts for the others."

"Ssh. They didn't expect you too." Justin squeezed his hand.

"But..."

"Don't worry."

Noel pulled in his lower lip and nibbled on it.

Soon, William and Jamie had passed out all of the gifts. Mini-piles were in front of everyone. Justin and Noel each had colorful piles of wrapped gifts.

"Okay, everyone, all presents exchanged. Tear into them!" William shouted.

Cries of pleasure rose and then the sounds of paper tearing filled the house. *Oohs* and *ahhs* started as goodies revealed and adored.

As he worked his way through the pile of gifts, Noel couldn't believe how many he received from the thoughtful guests. He loved all of his presents, each one chosen with care and knowledge of how he'd restarted his life in town with Justin.

"You dropped some hints about me on the Addicts newsletter, didn't you?" he asked Justin.

Justin gave him a little wince. "Yeah, I kinda did. Are you mad at me?"

"No, I know you did this because you care and so do they. Thank you."

"Anytime, dream boy." Justin pressed a kiss to his temple. "I love the pen and pencil set. It's wonderful."

"I'm sure you have numerous ones..."

"I actually lost my last set a few months ago and have been meaning to replace it," Justin admitted.

"You need to organize your desk."

"Gets crazy during the holidays, honest."

"Uh-huh. Right."

"I'll work on the organization thing."

Noel nuzzled his neck and kissed him. "Thank you for my gift. I love the leather wallet. After everything else you've given me..."

"Ssh. This is the holiday season and all you need to do is accept. I knew I couldn't give you the messenger bag I wanted."

Noel lifted his gaze to study him. "I think I'm ready for a new one." He fell quiet for the rest of the evening, leaning close to Justin.

Chapter Twelve

Rising on Christmas Eve after opening the generous mountain of birthday gifts with Justin taking notes of who had given him what and reassuring him, Noel stretched and saw snow falling out the bedroom window.

"Christmas snow," he said to the sleepy Marlowe.

The cat opened one amber eye before tucking his nose under the furry white-tipped tail.

Noel sat up and looked for the expected red envelope and found it.

On the 1st Day of Christmas, My One Hope Gave to Me:
Visions of the Season!
~ Secret Santa

"It's another mysterious message, Marlowe."

The feline didn't answer.

Not bothering with his morning routine or dressing, Noel rose from bed, took the message, and raced downstairs to the kitchen to find Justin. He found him flipping French toast on a platter and pulling brown sugar bacon from the oven.

"What's this one?"

Justin turned and grinned. "I did ask you to trust me a little more with these last few envelopes."

"Yeah, you did."

"Then please do this? Let's enjoy our Christmas Eve together?"

"Okay."

"Thank you." Justin stepped over to him, cupped his face, and placed a gentle kiss on his lips. "Merry Christmas Eve, Noel, and good morning."

"Merry Christmas Eve, Justin."

"Now, I want you to take your envelope, go back upstairs, and do your testing. Stay in your pajamas. It's all part of the message." Justin gave Noel a gentle swat on his ass to send him moving.

The day was spent in front of a roaring fire, the TV played various Christmas movies which had them laughing hysterically and *aww*-ing as families came together, tears falling at the classic scene of James Stewart running through the snow-strewn streets, shouting hello to all the beloved buildings and people of Bedford Falls until he found his family in *It's a Wonderful Life*.

"Okay, I love that one." Noel sniffled and wiped his eyes as it finished with everyone singing to James Stewart's character.

"Want another one?" Justin knelt in front of the media center as he popped out the DVD.

"Got some cartoons?"

"Classic ones. Rudolph, Santa, Frosty, and the Grinch," Justin said as he held them up.

Noel sipped on his hot cocoa. "Anyone of them is good, oh wait, the Grinch? Grinch!"

Justin chuckled and pulled out the animated version of *How the Grinch Stole Christmas*. He set it in the player and returned to Noel's side before hitting the play button.

"This is so much fun. I never had a day where I could veg in front of a TV and watch movies all day. Of course, one would need a TV to watch," Noel said as he curled against Justin's side.

"Are you enjoying the visions?"

"Yeah, I am. Good envelope message. I like how it's just us today."

"I had a feeling you could use a break after last night's party. We're going to William and Christina's home for Christmas dinner. The morning is for us to exchange gifts privately."

"Sounds good," Noel said as he snuggled closer to Justin.

Justin moved his fingers through Noel's hair. He shifted and drew Noel between his legs until he rested back against Justin's chest. He draped the Christmas throw over them.

"Want a pillow?" Justin offered.

"Nah, I'm comfortable like this. You don't mind?" Noel twisted his head to gaze up at Justin's face.

"No, this is perfect." Justin wrapped his arms low around Noel to keep them together.

Both cats appeared, meowed for attention, and leapt on the sofa to find places near them. Raleigh ended up on the back of the sofa near Justin's shoulder while Marlowe settled between their joined legs.

"Hey, buddy," Noel said as he scratched Marlowe's fuzzy head.

Justin nuzzled with Raleigh, who rubbed his face against Justin's unshaved cheek and purred loudly. "Now this is even better," Justin said.

"Yeah, the best holiday. Thank you for sharing it with me, Justin."

"More than welcome, Noel. I wouldn't have you go anywhere else."

Before they knew it, the peaceful, snow and movie filled day slipped into an evening filled with leftovers. While Noel watched Justin bank the fire for the night, he waited until they could climb the stairs together and part for separate bedrooms.

Justin brushed off his hands as he rose. "There we go. Should burn a few more hours with the last log and keep the house heated. Did you wait for me?"

Noel nodded and held out his hand. "After the wonderful day we shared, I didn't want it to end."

"Doesn't have to end. Come to my room and share my bed," Justin said while he stepped over to stand in front of him.

"I... Oh..."

"Ssh... Nothing more than sleep, I promise. I know it's only been a week."

Noel flushed. "You must think I'm a stupid dork or something."

"No more than me since I don't want to mess up what we're trying to start here."

"Are we trying to start something?"

"I sure do hope so, Noel."

"Then yes, I want to spend the night with you, nestled in your arms," Noel said as he lifted his gaze to meet Justin's gaze.

"All I ever wanted for Christmas this year was to gain your trust, friendship, and I hope a little bit more," Justin said, weaving their fingers together as they climbed the stairs.

The cats pranced ahead of them, fluffy tails waved back and forth.

This morning when Noel woke, he found himself wrapped in strong arms and snuggled against a wide chest. He felt a morning erection pressed against his pajama-covered ass.

Justin.

He was in Justin's bed, in Justin's room. As promised, they hadn't done anything beyond kissing and touching. Justin had been a complete gentleman. He insisted on waiting. He mentioned they'd known each other only a week and realized Noel felt uncomfortable about how reliant he was upon Justin's generosity and kindness.

Noel couldn't understand or believe how well the other man had read him so well. He adored Justin's consideration and old-fashioned tenderness. After all his time on the streets, he never had a relationship. Hell, he never had sex with a man. He had no idea what to do with

Justin, but knew he was in strong capable hands to see him through his first time.

"Hmm, you're awake," Justin said in a sleepy warm tone. He nuzzled and kissed the sensitive spot where Noel's shoulder and neck met.

"Merry Christmas." Noel twisted his head for Justin's kiss.

Justin's warm gaze met his and he smiled at Noel's words. "Merry Christmas," he whispered against Noel's lips.

"Part of me doesn't want to get up to open the last red envelope. I'm way too comfortable in your arms. Looks like a part of you doesn't want me to move either." He wiggled his ass against Justin's erection.

"Tempting brat, hold still or you'll pay for the deviation from our sworn rules." Justin clamped a hand on Noel's hip and pressed him into the mattress. A soft muttered curse left his lips as his erection hardened and lengthened.

"Hmm. Should I do it again?"

"No! You're going to get out of bed and follow me!" Justin ordered and managed to smack Noel's ass under the covers.

"Ow!" Noel shifted off the bed, rubbing the offended cheek, and stood. "You seem to have this weird thing about hitting my ass."

"I know. It's so bubbly and cute."

Noel lifted an eyebrow as he followed him out of the bedroom. "Are you into smacking lovers?"

"Perhaps, with the right ones. What about you?"

"Don't know."

Justin chuckled. "We'll leave it on the table for discussion at a later time."

Shoving fingers through his hair, the ends standing every which way by the time he was done, Noel stood on the bottom landing of the stairs and yawned. "Why did we get out of the warm bed? Other than you wanted to air out your morning wood a different way?"

Justin crossed his arms and glared at him.

"What? It's true."

"I forget, you've never had the chance to pounce on adults at the butt-crack of dawn, race downstairs to find what Santa brought for you, and tear into the paper to see all the gifts," Justin murmured.

"Nope," Noel said and popped the "p" sound.

"Shit."

"No big deal. Can't miss what you've never experienced."

"This whole week with the red envelopes was about giving you those special holiday experiences, Noel. The ones you missed growing up in the orphanage and group homes and years on the streets. I wanted to share them with you this year."

"Oh!"

"The first few were some necessity items that needed to be done. Except for the messenger bag, but we'll handle that change together."

Noel nodded, since he knew the time to replace it was coming.

"The rest were filled with seasonal traditions and surprises."

"And today?"

"Today is... Today's envelope is...special. Go and find it on the tree." Justin tilted his head to the tree.

"When did you hide it?"

"Santa left it."

Noel chuckled as he stepped off the landing and over a cat, which had to get in the way, and began to circle the tree. He noticed there were new wrapped gifts at the base. "How much shopping did you do beyond our day?"

"Enough."

"Sheesh. Buy out a store why don'tcha."

"Find the envelope."

There was a flash of red on one of the higher branches, the familiar envelope tucked in against the lights and an ornament.

He lifted on tiptoes and managed to get his fingers on the envelope. "Got it!" He pulled it down and turned it over to open the back. Noel slid the beautiful linen card from inside and read the message, a little different from all the others, and his eyes began to tear.

On Christmas Day, My True Love Gave to Me:
The Key to his Heart!
~ Love, Justin

Noel lifted his attention from the card to find Justin in front of him. He watched the man of his dreams, his safe haven from the snow and storms, open his hand to reveal a pair of small platinum keys on chains.

"One for you. One for me," Justin said. "I want us to promise each other a future. We pledge to give each other our hearts, souls, and love. We'll know with absolute certainty we can trust one another. When it's time, we can exchange them for rings and vows."

"I have nothing to give you," Noel said.

"You're everything I want in a partner, Noel. Sweetness hidden behind those protective walls, and loyalty, trust, and, I hope, your heart and love. I'll give you everything I am and more for all of this."

Noel flung his arms around Justin's neck and prepared to hold on to this man for the rest of their lives.

Dreamy...Sensual...Forever Love

A quiet one, Nicole Dennis is the penname of an asexual author of different genres of fiction – both LGBT+ and hetero. Lots of characters, worlds, and stories build up in her head until she must get them down on the screen – anything from romance to fantasy to paranormal.

During the day, she works in a quiet office in Central Florida, where she makes her home, and enjoys the down time to slip into her imagination. She is owned by a feline companion – a fluffy house panther, known as Midnight the Void. A very special furbaby who is FIV+ and polydactyl on her front paws (fluffy danger mittens!).

Contact & Media Info:

Website: http://nicoledennis.net

Email: nicoledennis.author@gmail.com

Facebook:

Main: www.facebook.com/NicoleDennis.Author

Page: https://www.facebook.com/NicoleDennis.Musings/

Group: https://www.facebook.com/groups/nicoledennis.author/

Amazon: https://www.amazon.com/author/nicoledennis

Threads: https://www.threads.net/@ndennis_author

Mastodon: https://mastodon.lol/@nicoledennis

QueeRomance: https://www.queeromanceink.com/mbm-book-author/nicole-dennis/

Goodreads: http://www.goodreads.com/author/show/ 2791975.Nicole_Dennis

Other Stories to Try

Entwined Publishing / Pride Publishing

Southern Charm

A M/M series based around the Southern Charm Bed and Breakfast located in a small Florida town on a barrier island below Pensacola. **Freebies available on my website or email for PDF**

Rules of the Chef
By the Numbers
On the Green
When in Bloom
Following the Law
According to Design
Saving the Wedding
Unexpected in the End (Coming Soon)

FatCat Books Ink

McShayne Bloodline

A fantasy quartet set in the Lands.

Magic passed through ancient bloodlines for generations. A powerful family gifted with a blend of Elf, Fae, and Human magic, the McShaynes watched over the balance of nature. While the Otherkin receded from any mortal connection, the McShaynes refuse to leave their ancestral lands. Until the humans turn against magic.

Four McShayne sons spread across the Lands. Each one fears he is the last. They fight to survive the harsh atmosphere, maintain their bloodline gifts, and discover love and the true meaning of family.

McShayne's Dragon
McShayne's Fae
McShayne's Elf

McShayne's Merman (Coming late 2025!)

Cheimon Tales
A new twist on tales from the North Pole.

Cracks in the Ice
Others coming soon

Lyon Lynx Clan
A paranormal series of Lynxes following the life of a newcomer, Derick Atwater.

Paws in the Snow
Others coming soon

Other Re-Releases:
Walk Me Trilogy
A M/M trilogy of love, life, and music from the boys of country-rock band, Midnight Twang.

Walk Me Down the Middle
Walk Me Through the Haze
Walk Me Through the Darkness

Built Piece by Piece
At the Masquerade
Mischief Corner Books:

Secrets & Silk

Siren Publishing: (BookStrand.com)
Grant's Mechanic (MM)
Unholy Angel (MF Erotic Paranormal)
Fire Jaguars (MMF Paranormal)

1 – Fire Moon Dance
2 – Luna Moon Dance
3 – Dark Moon Dance
Other books are in the works